TERROR ISLAND

SYAWAL

Table of Contents

CHAPTER 1

"Wake up Max. You're going to be late for your trip!"

Upon hearing his mother, Max took his time to get out of bed to prepare.

"Relax mom. We booked the ship ourselves. I highly doubt that they'll leave without us." Max shrugged, replying to his mother. "Besides, it's the holidays. We should cherish these moments before hell starts once again."

When he had finished preparing and went to have his breakfast, he was surprised to see his friends in the living room.

"Hey Max." Wilhem said after noticing Max coming down the stairs. Wilhem wore a blue cardigan with slim cut jeans, his hair all spiked up. For a moment, Max thought they were going out on a normal outing instead of a voyage to find the mysterious treasure.

"Has everyone arrived yet?" Max asked whilst looking at his watch.

"Almost everyone. Haley said she will meet us there

directly"

"That's Haley I suppose. That's the reason why we decided to meet an hour earlier" Max said while letting out a laugh.

Max went to the kitchen before turning to his friends. He wondered how this group of people had managed to stay close over the years. On the living room sofa, there was Sam who brought his laptop along for his studies. 'The internet is the key to our survival' – he once said.

"Anyways, the sea ain't going anywhere guys." Max said while going to the kitchen. "Have you guys eaten?"

"Yeah we ate before coming here. Come on Max. Treasures are waiting for us, waiting to be found."Jane, sitting beside John said, unable to contain her excitement. Dressed in a pink T-shirt and shorts, she stood up and began walking around the house. "Come to think about it, this is the first time I've been to your house Max"

"Give it a year or two and you'll know the contents of everything in Max's room"

"Okay fine, give me a few minutes more and we can set off."

Soon, the six of them packed their bags and after everything was settled, Max walked towards his mother and noticed his mother was looking worried. Even though he knew his mom would be worried, as he looked towards his mother's troubled face, his heart ached.

"Mom, it's going to be okay. I'll be back before you know

it." Max said before hugging his mother tightly as that was the only way he knew to comfort his mother. "I came back after the previous time, remember?"

"Max.... The last time you said that, you had wounds all over your body. In spite of those worrying times,it feels different now. Something feels different Max" his mother said, trying her best to hold back her tears. "Please promise me you will take care of yourself"

Max gave his word to his mother before giving her another hug. Despite him going on multiple trips before, this time his mom had truly tried her best to convince him to cancel his trip. "Besides, I'll have them with me"

When the car had turned a corner, Max looked back towards his mother. A tear fell as he saw his mother on her knees, cupping her face. He then made a promise to himself that he would be back in one piece and would bring a discovery so great that it would bring the smile back to his mother's face.

As soon as they got to the pier, they rushed towards the furthest end as the anticipation to look at their boat took over. It was a blue motor yacht boat, the length of 13 meters. It was as majestic as advertised. It stood there with pride, showing off its beauty to Max and his friends. They were satisfied with the accommodation. As they were busy admiring the exterior of the ship, a rugged man dressed in leather wearing a cap that had parts of it bitten off approached them. They almost mistook him as an actor for those pirate movies that they always watched.

"A thing of beauty, isn't she?" the rugged man asked.

"Bought her when she was nearing the end of her life and made some changes myself."

The group of six came back to their senses and nodded their heads, still admiring the ship.

"Name's Ory and I'm going to be your captain throughout the trip." Ory introduced himself to the group.

Max went up to Ory to introduce himself and his friends. Halfway throughout the introduction of the ladies in the group, for a minute and a second, Max noticed Ory giving off a smirk before returning to his smile. Max knew there was something wrong and wanted to call him out but he held himself back. He needed to gather more evidence. He decided not to warn his friends as that would only alert the captain. However, he also felt that that moment could be all his misunderstanding. After the pleasantries was done, Ory brought the group to tour around the ship, before letting them familiarize themselves with the interior of the ship. Max was impressed with the interior of the ship. The rooms were spacious with ample room space. They took about fifteen minutes settling down. Max took the room closest to the door as he could easily access the deck of the ship to know the situation. Max could not contain his excitement as the time for their adventure was close. The sea breeze beckoning them to venture forth.

As they were relaxing on board, they heard a girl's voice from a distance. Once the figure was nearing the ship, they went straight to the girl. Haley was panting by the time she reached the ship. She wore a yellow tank top, with blue hot pants along which seems to further accentuate her figure.

"Sorry guys, too many things to pack and too little time to do it. So I brought only the essential stuff that we need for our voyage" Haley said in between breaths, while pointing to the 4 luggage behind her that was carried by her butler. She took off her cartwheel hat to cool herself.

"Are you planning to go and never come back?" Max asked in disbelief trying to process the four huge bags now placed in front of them. "I think we'll most likely capsize halfway than to make it there safely."

"Max!" Haley gasped before continuing, "don't come begging when you're sunscreen's out" the group laughed and joked around before Max introduced her to the captain.

As soon as they helped Haley get settled on the boat, Max nodded towards the captain. The captain horned several times before setting sail. As they noticed the shore getting further and further away,reality sank in. They are going on their very first voyage.

The group of them decided to rest in the lounge area as they were still feeling the adrenaline pumping. They were discussing how they were going to spend the riches once they did find treasure. On the furthest side of the room, Sam was sitting on the bench, his attention solely on his laptop. Max was always amazed at how fast Sam's typing speed was. Not wanting to disrupt his friend's concentration, Max jsatthere for a while before heading back to the deck to view the ocean.

As he was gazing into the horizon, it took him a while

before he noticed Ory standing beside him.

"Y'know kid, the place you wanted to go, there is nothing there." Ory decided to break the awkward silence in the air.

"Then why'd you decide to take us then? Think it's easy to take advantage of us kids?" Max replied, looking towards the ocean instead of Ory.

"You really think that low of me huh kid. I decided to take you because you reminded me of myself when I was young. Wanting to go on adventures with my mates, enjoying life when we still could. But.." his voice trailed off.

Max looked at the captain but the captain looked away, avoiding his gaze. Unable to make out the captain's expressions, Max continued gazing towards the dark sky.

Max felt conflicted. What seemed to be sincerity from the captain's might be a façade to throw him off the trail. The captain was not wrong in one part. Everyone told him that there was nothing in the place that he was looking for. Max was tempted to believe them and cancel the whole thing but his gut feeling prevented him from doing so. There was something in that place. At this moment, he also felt warmth in the gestures of his friends. They could have not only rejected the idea of Max going alone, giving him plenty of excuses but they even went along instead. He knew he could not let anything happen to his friends and that was why he had to keep his guard up around the captain. His only wish was that they manage to find whatever was there and return safely. Max returned back to his room to try and get some sleep in before they reached their destination.

CHAPTER 2

'Thud!'

Max was flung from his bed, crashing his head on the floor. His head stinging with pain,he looked around and saw everything was moving rapidly and without rhythm. With much effort, he managed to find his balance and began treading towards the deck with the help of the walls and handles. As he opened the door, he was hit with an outburst of air smashing unto his face. It was lucky that he was gripping the handle on the door, otherwise he would have lost his balance and could have incurred heavier injuries. Suddenly, Max heard his friends screaming. With a storm going at it with her might, after much squinting, he could finally see what was causing the commotion. It did not take long as he was hit with splashes from the ocean. He looked around and saw John, struggling with the wheel. Max quickly went to John's side to help.

The winds were howling as hard as it could, trying to topple anything in its path.

"Where's the captain John"

"Beats me. When I woke up, it was already a disaster. I

didn't go to the captain's quarters as this is much more important. I didn't know steering a ship could be so hard!" John exclaimed, competing with the noise of the storm. Max could now see that John was using everything he had to steer the wheel. Veins were bulging on his arms as he held the wheel in place.

Max and John struggled as best as they could. Things were sliding everywhere. Max watched the items being hurled overboard, there was nothing that could have been done to retrieve them. It was like an obstacle course with the items being flung around. Thunder kept roaring in the skies, trying to exert its dominance. It was as if there was a ferocious battle in the sky. Lighting kept making their appearances, illuminating the sky with their brilliance. Bolts of white protruded the dark and gloomy skies, it treated the sky as its canvas. Max was not sure of how this was going to end. He could only hope that they would be able to survive this ordeal safely. The sea kept rising, towering over them as if looking down on them. As if the water was taking their rage out on them, unforgiving and turbulent. Then it came crashing down on the struggling boat, trying its best to capsize the boat. When the water hit, the group was flung around. His head was hit against the side, Max tried to stand up with the help of the railings. Before long, the next wave hit them once again. Gasping for air, Max tried desperately to struggle back to the steering wheel.

"Max! The weather is getting worse. Do we head back or…" John said while crawling towards him, his face showing signs hoping that Max would choose to return.

Max knew he should choose to return but the destination stumped him. He was unsure of their location and even if he chose to return, which direction do they head towards. With the captain gone, he could not navigate towards the sea as he was inexperienced enough.

He looked towards John and shook his head. "We push through! We're too far in to know where we are and I believe that if we continue moving forward, we can survive through this weather."

John looked at him for a few seconds before nodding, "Though I knew you were going to say that, I kinda hoped you went a different direction."

The battle between the ship and the storm was similar to that of tug of war. Neither side wanted to lose.Water levels kept rising while Haley and Wilhem kept chugging water off the boat. Their faces were weary and their arms were crying in pain, but they knew if they stopped or stopped for a while that it would not only sink the ship, it would leave them swimming in the middle of nowhere trying to survive the dangers of the ocean. The group of them had the same question buzzing – when was the storm ever going to subside.

Out of a sudden, the group was bathed in sunlight. The rain was nowhere to be seen. Each of them slumped to the ground. They were exhausted, gasping for air after the intense battle. They looked at each other, trying to sound words but none seemed to make a sound. Their throats were sore from all the shouting. Some of them cried, mostly feeling relieved they had managed to survive. A few of them had started to give up hope as they could not hold on any longer. That was the first time in their lives that they had to face something of that calibre. Max shivered as he started to think about his journey back. Alas, there was so little he could do. He decided to take things one step at a time. Now, his goal is to move forward and venture on to discover the hidden island for the treasure. Only by finding it would it make the whole trip and their sufferings worth it.

Max woke up after a while. His body was filled with pain and he struggled to stand. He limped on towards his room. Out of nowhere, an arm rested on his shoulder.

"Hey boy. Nasty storm isn't it? It may be due to some sort of luck but we managed to survive eh!" the captain said while laughing.

"We?! What is all this "we" stuff? Before that, where were you? What we needed was you. You, the captain, who had a ton of experience with disasters like that and you're not even there! What did we hire you for?" Max shouted with rage. So much pent up emotion in him, he vented out on the captain. He thought that the captain would take the lead, steer them through the storm but alas all his expectations were crushed.

The captain shrugged his shoulders. "I was tending to all your items, kid. I was checking to see if anyone needed help in your rooms." The captain tried to reason with Max along the lines, his eyes kept staring anywhere but Max's.

Max looked at the captain in disbelief. Thoughts kept running through his mind but he could not voice them out. He was in utter shock at the captain's answers. Too tired to continue the argument, Max turned around and headed straight towards his bed. All he desperately need now is to lie down and sleep somewhere more comfortable than his previous place.

The ship sailed smoothly forward, giving Max and his friends a comfortable rest as if rewarding them. Max stretched his arms, having enjoyed a good sleep. He walked towards the deck of the ship. Max realised the ship had stopped moving. He saw John at the helm holding binoculars.

"Why did we stop, John." Max asked.

John turned towards Max, handed him the binoculars and answered, "You would want to see this for yourself."

Max took the binoculars and pointed it towards the area John was looking at. He was surprised. In his view stood an island. Somewhere towards the front of the island, there appears to be an abandoned port, made of wooden planks and there lies torn flags on the poles. Furthermore, there were many boats that were wrecked. Max gazed towards the island with feelings of excitement.

"Did you reckon we have found it?" John broke the silence to ask Max.

Max looked at John and nodded, "I think we did John, I think we did."

John broke the news to the rest of the group. They decided to celebrate and rest the night, to gain their energy before heading towards the island. Perhaps they had watched too many movies, but it would not hurt to be prepared for the adventure that is to come.

CHAPTER 3

Once Max stepped onto the pier, it gave a soft creak. The appearance of the pier showed that it had not been used for a long time. They each alighted cautiously, fearing that the pier might crumble. As there appears to be wooden shards around the pier, even if the water is shallow, the shards might leave unwanted injuries. They treaded carefully until they reached solid ground. They each heaved a sigh of relief as from the way the creak sounded, it was warning them that one misstep could very well cost them their lives. Max then looked up and what was in front of him sent shivers down his spine. It was a massive jungle that gave off an eerie feeling. They stared towards the mouth of the jungle. Even though it was pitch black, it was enticing them to enter.

Jane dropped to her knees, as if trying to hide from someone.

"Jane!" John and Haley exclaimed, rushing to her sides and trying to help her up. As they were helping her stand, she was struggling to find her footing, her body trembling and slowly recovering from shock.

Max took off his backpack and offered Jane to sit as an alternative to a chair. Wilhem, on the other hand, handed her a bottle of water to calm her down.

“Jane, are you okay?” Max kneeled beside Jane and inquired. He is worried about the condition of his friend.

All Jane did was nod towards him. She was gasping for air, feeling as though someone had choked her. She wanted to crawl into her ball, trying to escape from whatever that was there.Her face white as the driven snow.

“Calm down Jane. We’re right beside you.” The group of four tried consoling Jane. This was the first time Jane had ever shown this type of fear.

Once Jane had calmed down, she looked towards the group of people. “Max, this..this jungle is different. One minute I was with you guys and the next, I was stuck in darkness Max. At first, there…There…was…nothing but blood all around me.. Then, I saw them.” She covered her face. She took a few more breaths. “Eyes... Staring at me.” Tears began to fall down her face. They quickly hug her, to provide her with a sense of security.

Max looked towards the entrance. He pondered for a few minutes. He then looked towards John and asked him to stay behind with Jane as she was in no condition to travel. The reason behind this is to allow Jane time to recover while they quickly explore the jungle. After a minute second, John agreed to Max's plan. It was better for one person to stay with Jane to provide her with the company while the rest explore part of the jungle. This may have sounded cruel but they had to do this so that they can finish the expedition faster to get Jane home. This is to allow them to have a better understanding of the island and provide them with a clue as to the history of the island. After they had done setting camp, Max and the rest divided themselves into two separate groups. Just as they were about to set off, Jane ran to the front of the group, halting them. She pleaded to join the group, proceeded to explain that she did not want to drag the team down and she wanted to at least contribute. They looked at each other and smiled before looking back at her. Even though they knew she would want to join, they could not help but show concern towards her. With that, they decided to enter the jungle as a group as they would achieve a sense of security with everyone present.

They followed what seemed to be a pathway deep into the jungle. Max was hoping there to be traces of civilization as it would at least provide them clues to treasures. The jungle seemed to have a life on its own. The sound of birds and crickets created a symphony which beckoned them deeper, and they were dancing to nature's tunes. The pathway began to loom further. The trees stood beside the pathway, seemingly inviting the group to walk in further. The further they venture in, the less they can see. As they were focusing on staying on the path, the less they realised that it was getting dark. For what seemed like eternity, they came across an open land. They were saved from having to endure the horrors of the forest, from the harsh bites of the insects, the eerie call of the forest along with the heavy atmosphere. They were marvelled at the sight before them.

It appeared to be remnants of a village, creating a grand scenery standing before them. Wilhem took a step forward, bent down and began inspecting the ground. Max looked at him, then proceeded to delve in further into the village, trying to figure out the scene. He came up to a house that was bigger compared to the other houses. The houses in the village were circular in shape, each of the houses trying to indicate that they were built in the ancient era. The houses had stone bricks as the walls and straw hays as rooftops. It was surprising to him as this house was one of the two houses that had stood against the test of time and remained standing. Part of Max was delighted as this could be their chance to uncover history that might lead to their big break in life. Max approached the house and noticed writings on the stone walls. Max glanced at the wordings before proceeding on as he was not affluent in foreign languages. Instead of getting hung up on the ancient language, he proceeded towards the entrance of the house. He pushed slightly on the door before the door collapsed backwards, pushing up dust all around. Taking a step back and brushing off all the dust off himself, Max entered the house. The house was a complete mess. A large stone chair was placed right at the centre of the circle. The chair gave off a grandiose feeling, with the light seemingly focused on the chair. It gave off a majestic vibe leading Max to assume that it was built for a leader. As he headed towards the chair, he tripped and landed on his chest. It was then that Max noticed that there were writings of the same language written on the floor. Max stood up and followed the writing. Starting from the entrance, the writings ended at the foot of the chair. On the backseat of the stone chair, there was a single word that was written in bold. Max took a wild guess and assumed that it meant the word "Leader" given the setting of the room. He also assumed that the writings on the floor were some sort of record. He decided he would leave this to Wilhem as Wilhem was more proficient compared to him. He continued looking around the house, trying to find anything that might stand out in the room. As he was roaming around the room, he felt as though he was being watched. The feeling intensified the moment he stepped closer to the chair. The chair seemed like it was beckoning him to touch it. Feeling curious, Max proceeded to place his hand on the arm rest of the chair.

Without warning, the chair lit up. Max felt a warm sensation flowing through him, starting from his hand to the rest of his body. When Max no longer felt the sensation anymore, the chair dimmed, losing its light whilst giving off a low hum. Max was mesmerised by the whole process and when he came to, the chair was in pieces. This piqued his interest as this proves that magic might be real and used in the ancient times. Realising that there was nothing else he could do, he continued to search the room.

After a long search around the room, his search was unsuccessful. The room was filled with debris and no matter which rock Max turned over, it only uncovered more rocks. With the state of the room, it was evident that the occupant of the room at that time took everything with them except for the chair. Max was partly disappointed as he wanted there to be at least a sign for him to find a valuable item. Not wanting to waste anymore time on an empty search, Max called in Wilhem to investigate the wordings on the floor. As soon as Wilhem entered the room, his eyes lit up and went straight to work. Wilhem took out his magnifying glass and went to inspect the wordings on the floor.

Wilhem was profusely shaking his head. "This is… a language that I have never seen before. From the structure of the words, it seems to focus on the word *khatar*." Wilhem explained. "Give me this afternoon and i will get back to you what it says."

Max nodded as he turned to look towards the horizon. It was getting dark and it would take hours to return to the ship. Just as he was about to reply, they heard a shriek outside. They both ran to the source of the shriek. They dashed into the other hut and saw Haley on the ground. She had tripped upon stepping on an object before the object gave way, making her lose her footing. Max and John stood by her sides to help her up. It was then that Max noticed that she had an object in her left hand and asked her about it. As she brought the item into view, it was a shape of a skull.

"At first, i thought this was a normal human skull. However, upon closer inspection, this person had been too much." Haley said, while proceeding on to point at several areas of the skull. "Look at these areas. These are not fall damages, it was done by something much worse. I do not know what might have caused these injuries, but i would imagine that it was something fearsome."

"Maybe it was made by a wild animal in that period of time maybe?" John said.

"Perhaps. It must be one heck of an animal to incur this type of injury." Haley replied, while examining the skull.

Seeing that it was getting dark soon, they decided to camp at the village. They sat in a circle to discuss their findings. It turns out that there was close to nothing in the village. The only highlights of their day was the discovery of the foreign language and the skeleton remains of a person. Even though it was not much, Max felt relieved that they at least managed to find an item or two.

They set up camp inside the hut as it provided them the shelter in case it rained. It was better to continue exploring the area that day. Max was just about to sleep before he was dragged in by darkness. He called out to his friends but to no avail. It was as if he was the only one in darkness. He tried running around but his feet would not listen to him. He was rooted to the ground. He tried many different actions but was met with resistance. He clenched his heart. He saw a speck of light approaching. However, the speck of light brought with it a threatening feeling. As the light got closer, fear kept rising in Max. Before the light reached him and disappeared, it let out multiple huge roars. Max stumbled when he felt a hand on his shoulder.

"Max, are you okay?" John assisted him before asking.

Max was sweating profusely. He looked at John before checking his surroundings. Seeing that it was all back to normal, he nodded towards John before replying.

"Yeah...Yeah, I'm fine thanks. Must be the exhaustion catching up to me or something."

Max understood John's worried facial expression. Both Jane and him were experiencing paranormal activities. It was challenging to explain to the rest as it all happened instantly and to comprehend all of it was close to impossible. What was important to them now was a good night's rest so that they can continue their exploration on this weird island.

CHAPTER 4

Max kept twisting and turning, he felt as though he was being chased. His hand felt as though it was caught on fire. He felt that something was out to get him but he was not sure what. He was sweating profusely when he finally saw them. Two figures standing stood before him, just staring. They were wearing the sort of tunic found in ancient times. Max could hardly make out their faces as the darkness was overwhelming his eyesights. His instincts told him to run, however, he told himself that since this might not be real, he could try communicating with these people. As he was about to ask them, they shouted multiple words that he could not understand.

"*Yarkud! Khatar!*"

They kept shouting over and over, hoping for Max to understand. Max then felt an eerie feeling on his back. Slow and calm breaths could be heard. Looking at the two's expressions from earlier, Max could roughly guess the situation he was in. He turned his head to look at the source of the eerie feeling. His heart stopped, his eyes widened with fear. What was staring at him was eyes that were scarlet red that could swallow him and drown him in the world of darkness. Saliva was drooling from the creature's mouth. He tried to run but to no avail as the creature held Max in place. The creature then uttered a few words which Max could understand.

“We... will... be.... waiting,boy.” it said. It’s voice sounded coarse. It was struggling to utter those words as if it had never spoken for a very long time. It tapped Max’s head before Max woke up sitting.

He was drenched from head to toe. He looked around and saw that his friends were still sleeping. He checked his watch and that was when he noticed the bruises on his arms. It was the exact location as where the creature had held him in place. It was almost dawn. Max could not bear to sleep after what had just happened. He walked out of the building to get some fresh air. Bringing a flashlight and a change of clothes, he went to check out the surroundings to find a source of water,preferably a lake. His body felt sticky and he was in desperate need of a shower. After walking for about half an hour, he finally found a lake. He could not help but shout for joy as this was one the breaks he needed. Without hesitation, he took off all his clothes and went straight in to shower. It took him quite a while to shower, he wanted to be fresh and wash all his troubles away. After showering, he wore his clean clothes and proceeded back to where his friends were.

His friends were already awake by the time and were chatting amongst themselves. Haley, who saw Max approaching, went up to him and gave him a quick glance.

“You went for a bath, didn't you?” she asked.

Max nodded towards her.

“No fair. I wanted to shower too!” she pouted.

“Alrights. Gather your things to shower.” Max said. Max then led them to the lake. Just before reaching the lake, they separated into ladies and gents to take turns showering. The girls went first by sprinting to the lake. Hence the guys could only find a place further from the lake to wait for the girls to be done with their shower.

Once everyone had settled, they returned to the building to rest for a bit before starting the day. Wilheim walked up to Max and pulled him aside. He took out a rough sketching from his backpack before motioning Max to sit beside him. Max looked at the rough sketchings and noticed that the contents was the language written in the building.

“Max, sorry but i’d reckon you would want to hear this without the presence of the rest.” Wilheim looked at him and said. His face was weary, most probably from staying up and trying to decipher the languages written.

Max nodded his head and allowed Wilheim to continue.

“I have racked my brain on this and i think this language is Arabic. However, the way it is written, it is probably not used today. The writings on the floor were records of a serious event that led them to run for their lives. It stated several hoards chasing them, consuming them at an ungodly speed. Though some of the words have been lost, it sounded like a calamity had befallen them. They mentioned that they were running away after the calamity. This last bit here.”

Wilhem pointed to the line near the end of the page and said, "This segment was written in bold. It said that there was nothing they could do. They mentioned that when travel was done in a single day, music to be heard right in the ears and technology so advanced it was small that they could manage to overcome the calamity. That was all I could decipher." Wilhem explained to Max.

Max looked at Wilhem before standing up and said,"Thanks Wilhem. That was actually quite impressive. I take it that the calamity has ended given that it happened hundreds of years ago?"

"Yeah… Oh and I also have the translation for the word on the chair. It stands for danger in arabic. The word has been mentioned several times in the records."

After hearing what Wilhem had uncovered, Max was curious. He wanted to find out the prison that was mentioned in the records. Max believed that the calamity was over and there were artefacts to be found. He did not mention the dream to his friends as he believed that even though it seemed real, it was just a nightmare and there lies no meaning behind it. Furthermore, he did not want paranoia to run in the group as that would hinder their progress. Putting that at the back of his mind, he decided to rejoin his friends. They had finally done uncovering the village and only managed to find the records of significant value. Wilhem took several sketches and pictures of the records and placed it in his backpack.

They moved out of the village to head northwards. There was no reasoning behind the direction as they agreed that travelling in a straight line was simple and efficient. Plus, it provides them with the direction back to their ship in any case of emergency. However, the path ahead consists of many obstacles such as hills that require them to scale both upwards and downwards, thick bushes that are too strong to be cut down and unpredictable terrain that could halt their progress. They had covered quite a distance before they stumbled upon a campsite. There were a total of five tents built all around the place. Armored men were patrolling around the place. The armored men were wearing gears unknown to Max and his friends.

"You think we should at least say hi to them?" Hayley said, breaking the silence between them.

Max and the others looked at her, each pondering further on her question. There should be no harm in greeting them but Max fears that it might backfire on them instead. If they are here on peaceful terms, there would be no need for that much firepower. Since they do not know the intentions of the armored group, they unanimously decide on observing the group further. There was no harm in observing further as this would affect their safety as a group.

"Maybe you should greet them. I'm sure they would not mind it at all." A voice that sounded deep that had a tone that could command beckoned them to turn their heads towards it. It came from a masculine man, his face had a scar across his face as if he got slashed horizontally from one ear to the other. He wore black overalls and was sitting on a boulder, his expression deadly. He looked at them before snapping his figures. Armored men appeared behind bushes and branches, pointing their guns at them with each of them having a smile on their face anticipating the command to shoot. Max was terrified and did not know what to do.

John slowly walked to the front of the group to try negotiating with the masculine man.

“Hi sir, me and my friends are here on a vacation. We assure you we will leave this place if you release us. No one will know you are here.” John tried his best to assure the man with every reason possible.

The masuline man raised his eyebrows and laughed. His hysterical laugh was so erratic that it sounded like someone was scraping steel. He shook his head and motioned towards the gunmen. The gunmen lowered their weapons. However, each of them looked heavily disappointed and walked away from them, all except one particular gunman who walked behind the masculine man. He stood at attention and looked blankly at Max and his friends, devoid of all expressions.

“Dear me. Where was my manners? Name’s Ashfaq and this here is my most loyal retinue, Klivert." The masculine man stood up and introduced themselves to Max and his friends.

“To be honest with you, we do not like to kill people. So please don’t give us a reason to.” Ashfaq continued. “You must be tired from your journey here. I am positive it was not a breeze to come to his island. Come, let us eat in my tent.”

Ashfaq led them to the largest tent that was different from the rest given the decoration it had. He mentioned that the reason it came to be was to differentiate from the rest. Max and his friends walked timidly to Ashfaq's camp. The gunmen were staring intensely enough that they could pierce them in their heart with their eyes. As they got closer to Ashfaq's camp, Max felt his hand burning up. He waved his hands to cool his hands down. Max saw further down, there lies the debris of a downed helicopter. Max knew that it was a chinook helicopter as it was a transport that could transport this many people. The helicopter was missing its tail, assuming as though it had been through a tough battle trying to reach the island. Max could roughly guess that these groups had no alternatives to exit this island to return to where they came from.

"Welcome to my humble abode." Ashfaq opened the curtains to his camp. He looked at them with a smile on his face. Max and his friends reluctantly went in as they had no other choice.

The tent was spacious with a bed located on his left and a resting area on his right. Max could see that this was a better accommodation than what he had thought. Ashfaq guided their attention towards the television and said that it could not work as the island does not have any reception. Then, Ashfaq led them to a long dining table, which was prepared with lascivious foods.

"Sit down my friends. These are foods made by the best people in their fields. It certainly was a challenge... acquiring them." Ashfaq said.

Max and his friends were famished as they were walking a

distance and not had any lunch yet. Their hunger gave them away and they quickly took a seat. They gobbled down their food whilst talking to Ashfaq. The girls were more receptive compared to the guys. Not long after, they were comfortable talking with Ashfaq.

"So, what were you guys actually doing on this island?" Ashfaq finally asked them.

Without hesitation, Haley told him the purpose of their visit. Ashfaq was surprised by Haley's quick honesty. His questions led to the direction of their objectives and whether they had made any significant discoveries. It was as if he was trying to find out more about what they were doing on the island. Max tried to answer casually without hinting at any sorts. He only just knew Ashfaq and he would not spill any sort of secrets. Even though Ashfaq was kind enough to offer them food and shelter, Max was not foolish enough to fall for it. Maybe that was all his paranoia but he could not be sure what the other was truly thinking. Not long after, his friends all had warmed up to Ashfaq. Giggles and laughter sounded throughout the table. Max decided to take a breather and left the tent. He noticed a particular behavior from the gunmen. Their attention was turned towards a certain direction every few seconds as if they were anticipating something. Max tried looking in the same direction but all he saw was the lush trees. He was given the cold shoulder every time he tried interacting with the guards. Knowing he could get nowhere, he decided to walk back to where his friends were. As soon as he had reached the tent, Ashfaq had already assigned his friends and him a place to sleep for the night. Apparently, they had already decided to join together to search for the treasures on the island as two groups are better than one. Or so he was told.

CHAPTER 5

Ashfaq sent one of his men to guide the kids to their resting area for the night whilst he retreated back to his chair. It was certainly exhausting trying to entertain kids while not thinking of disposing them. He was surprised to see there were other people on this island, especially kids their age. He spent a few minutes, concocting ways of how to handle the kids. Maybe it would be best to have them around to have a fresh perspective on the island. He had been there for a month and was not progressing as he would have liked. However, he had to be patient. When he took a glance at the kids, none of them stood out. They were probably telling the truth about not having found anything yet. Everyone except the boy, Max who hesitated before agreeing with his pal. He has garnered enough experience in life to know that Max was hiding something not just from him. As he was busy deciding on how to acquire the necessary information from Max, he sensed Klivert approaching from the back.

"Sir, we have investigated and noted everything in this report." Klivert passed Ashfaq a report then proceeded to stand further away from Ashfaq, waiting for Ashfaq to dismiss him.

Ashfaq nodded his head and allowed Klivert to leave the tent. From the report, it seemed that the group came from the south. It was quite a distance that they had travelled. They discovered a run-down village which one of the huts was used as a gathering for meetings from the way it had been decorated. What was more interesting to him was the picture of the broken chair located in the centre of the room. It was interesting as it seemed as though the way the chair broke happened naturally. Compared to the rest of the hut whereby they were trashed around. It reported that they had their boat docked further down the island in the abandoned pier. There was also a picture of their captain which intrigued him. He felt as though he had seen the captain before but did not exactly when or where. Deciding not to ponder on it further, he placed the report on the report on the table and leaned back on his chair. Several thoughts crossed through his mind. He stood up and headed straight for the exit. He needed to see the chair. He needs to find clues about this island and the thing that could lead to a discovery is the chair. It could be a breakthrough for him as he was at a loss of why they could not find anything for so long. Before leaving, he stationed two of his men to guard the group in case they suspected anything.

The journey took him a few minutes as he was in a hurry. He could not delay it any longer as he feared any clues might be gone over time. When he reached the destination, he darted straight for the hut with the broken chair. There he saw it, the chair that was once stood up with all the magnificence now lay broken on the floor. He could feel it inside him, there was something else in this room. He ordered the men to search more in this room, to uncover any untouched places to see if there was anything hidden. His men made a mess out of place. Throwing the non-essentials outside, feeling every part of the hut and digging every corner of the floor.

After what seemed like eternity, one of his men called up to him and pointed to his hole. Ashfaq ran to him and was ecstatic upon what his man had dug up. It was a small wooden box. He opened the box and saw that the box contained an old parchment. He took out the parchment and opened it. The content of the box gave him excitement as it was finally the first step forward. The blood written parchment did not shock or surprised him one bit as this was common in his line of work. It states that there lies a prison deep inside a mountain located at the west side of the island. The prison was said to hold a danger to the world. A danger that would consume anything that stood in its path. Before he could analyze the parchment further, another one of his men called out, holding another piece of parchments in his hands. He took the parchment and opened it. Similar to the first parchment, this was also written in blood. However, the content piqued his interest. In this parchment, it states of treasures that could not be grasped by the hands of men. These treasures were large in quantity and said to be guarded by beasts that could not be swayed by any forms of persuasion or coercion. These beasts were ferocious and would tear man apart, eating them to fuel itself.

Asfaq was intrigued by the two contents. He was more interested by the second than the first due to the mention of treasures. Despite the mentioned treasures, he could not discard the first parchment easily. He was deep in thought as to why there were two letters with different contents. There was one common mention in the two parchments that it represents a pandora box. He wanted to uncover what the prison or treasure is and this could be his ticket to greatness.

He looked back towards the chair and had a feeling that one of the kids might have something to do with breaking it. As it was also part of the room, he felt that there was a connection between all the three items. He decided to wrap things up and return back to his tent whereby they could prepare to journey towards the west and find more about the 'prison'.

As he walked towards his tent, he still could not calm his feelings. Multiple feelings are swimming in his heart, all trying their best to burst out. He had ordered his men to rest early as tomorrow will be a big day, whereby they have to be on alert on any instances that could jeopardise their mission. He would use the kids until he was sure they had little to no value, to which then he could dispose of them. Since he was unsure of what Max had seen or touched, he was sure Max had inherited the true meaning of the chair. He would continue to probe further into Max, and for that, he would spare Max's friends for now. He knew that threatening them would not work as it incurs heavy backlash. He had sacrificed too much just to reach this island.

CHAPTER 6

Max woke up to the loud engine sounds outside. It sounded as though the whole troop were preparing to move and he wondered what would happen to him and his friends. Max changed into a sports outfit and went outside to take a look. Indeed, the gunmen were packing the tents efficiently and within several minutes, they were done. He walked towards one of the gunmen and asked where they were headed. The gunman looked at him and shrugged before answering that they were headed somewhere in the west where Ashfaq believes there to be a breakthrough discovery. Max thought to himself whether they should follow Ashfaq. Following them might be great as he could share in the glory of discovering what was hidden. However, he was not sure about whether Ashfaq would be willing to share the glory as it would be illogical.

"It's Max,right?" he turned his head towards the voice at the mention of his name. He saw Ashfaq standing there with his arms folded. He nodded his head, trying to anticipate what would Asfaq say next.

"Care to join us to the west?" Ashfaq asked him.

Max was surprised at his question. Was he really willing to bring kids that he only just met to share his possible discovery of a lifetime? Though it did not really make sense to Max, he quickly nodded his head as to prevent Ashfaq from changing his mind. Furthermore, he would guarantee the safety of his friends with the presence of the heavy gunfire that Ashfaq has.

Max looked at Ashfaq's attempt at showing him a smile. Without dwelling on it too much, he went back to check on his friends. His friends had all woken up and are chatting amongst themselves. Haley looked at Max as he was entering the camp and asked him what their next step should be. Max gathered his friends in a circle to discuss their future. He told them briefly about what had happened to him when he experienced the strange light from the chair and his interactions with Asfaq that happened moments ago. His friends all looked to him, as if prompting him to make a decision for the whole group as they did not mind any decision he took. He stared at them, kind of expecting this reaction as he had known them for seven years and counting. His friends were the type that would follow him as they are worried about him. They were also the type that would hold nothing back at scolding him if the decision he made was wrong but that only happened once and Max had learnt that lesson the hard way.

Wilheim adjusted his glasses and said, “We do not mind any decision you make Max. We know you chose the one that is safest amongst them all. Just know that you are not alone.” He patted Max on the shoulder. With that, they had all packed up their things and were ready to leave, giving Max a surprise as he had yet to share his thoughts yet.

"I figured you would want to join them in their expedition hence I told the rest to pack things up and be ready to leave when you say so." John said. Max smiled, looked at his friends and motioned them to leave the tent together.

As they exited the tent, one of the gunmen was already waiting for them. Once he saw the group of six approaching,he turned and instructed them to get onto one of the humvees prepared for them. Max was curious as to where they are headed next. It was an uncomfortable trip as not only did they have to share their seats with some of the gunmen, they had to endure the bumps on the road which would randomly jerk the humvee.

'The island is bigger than I expected it to be..' Max thought to himself. He gazed through the window of the humvee, trying to take in the beauty of the forest. He saw different kinds of wildlife, each trying to coexist with one another to survive. He then turned to look towards the gunmen. It seemed that they had never caught a break. They looked concentrated, their face void of any emotion. Max wanted to strike a conversation but was met with resistance every time, ruining his plans of seeking answers as to why they were there. After a while, he grew bored and began talking to his friends, killing the time as they were told it was quite a distance.

The journey was interesting to Max as he watched Ashfaq stopping every few kilometers, surveying the island. He was searching for something as he kept investigating the terrain. Max wanted to assist him but was denied. By this point, the heat in his palm had spread throughout his entire hand. He understood that as they travel more to the west, the heat intensifies and spreads from his hand. He kept trying to cool his hands but to no avail. As they travel further, Ashfaq's reaction gets more elaborate and he kept grinning. It seemed to Max that they were getting closer to their destination. He felt that they were being contained for some reason as they could not disembark everytime they took a quick stop. The reason they were given was that it was to be efficient and by alighting would consume time that could have been saved. Max and his friends were in no position to argue as they were mismatched in terms of firepower. Hence, they had to endure sitting uncomfortably, with the unrelenting heat, praying to reach their destination as quickly as possible.

Max was getting sore as the hour passed. He glanced at his friends who were all wearing the same expressions. They desperately needed to alight to allow their blood to circulate and grant their bodies momentary freedom. They did not have to wait long as when they had to stop for the umpteenth time, the gunmen mentioned them to alight the vehicle. They rejoiced as they stepped down from the vehicle. They had to take a few moments to restart the motor of their legs as the needles were constantly poking.

Max surveyed his surroundings and saw that they were facing a great mountain looming over them. It's shadow provided them comfort and shelter from the burning rays of the sun. It seemed to span from one end to the other, it was different from its kinds. The mountain seemed to be inviting the group but it lacked an entrance. Ashfaq instructed his men to check if there were any signs of entrance to the mountain. After a few futile attempts, Max overheard Ashfaq wanting to create their own entrance. One of the men ran back to the humvee parked all the way at the back. Moments later, he came back with a rocket-propelled grenade launcher. Max was slightly impressed by the preparations of Ashfaq, though it was overkill. They retreated a distance before Ashfaq nodded towards the gunman.

Though they expected it, experiencing it first hand was something else. The blast was overwhelming to Max and his friends. They felt it resonate within their bodies, making some of their knees wobble. Trying their best to recover, they shifted their attention towards the impact point. It surprised the whole group as not a single dent was made. The mountain stood there, still in one piece tempting them to try again. The gunman fired again to try and make some kind of progress thinking it was impossible for it to survive a second strike. Once the dust and smoke had settled, they were still in disbelief. The second strike was similar to that of the first. Both did not inflict any damage to the mountain.

Max winced in pain moments after the second strike hit. He grabbed his hands, trying to alleviate the pain in his hands. It came abruptly causing Max to lose his footing. He tried to regain his footing, limping towards a nearby tree. He could not describe it but something deep inside was telling him to withdraw himself and get as far away from the mountain as possible. However, they were too invested to back away now. Max tried to bury the feelings away, enduring the pain and headed towards the mountain. For every step he took forward, the stinging pain intensified. He tried to keep a calm face as he would not want to worry his friends. John and Haley stood beside him, each holding both of his arms to support him. He looked at them and knew instantly that they were aware of his struggles.

"When did you know?" He asked.

John looked at Haley then back at Max. "Since we left the village."

They had walked until they were facing the mountain at arms length. The pain in his arms had subsided. He did not know what had caused the pain to subside. He began to question the reality of magic.

'Was magic all but an illusion?' He thought to himself.

As he was facing the rocks of the mountain, he began to reach out his hands to touch them. The mountain was beckoning him, calling out to him as if welcoming him back. Almost as if he was in a trance, he touched the mountain and said.

"Ana Asif"

The mountain suddenly shook vigorously. It felt as though an earthquake had struck, the deafening noise struck fear in their hearts. Each of them were clueless to the cause. The shakings and the rumblings went on for a minute but to them, it felt as though it would never end. They hugged the ground as best as they could. The relief they felt was indescribable and some slumped back in relief that they had managed to bear through. However, mixed feelings of shock and surprise overtook them as they laid their eyes on the mountain. Greeting them was an entrance of impenetrable darkness. It stood there naturally as if it had always been there. Max stood there as he broke out of his trance.

'What happened? What did I just say?' Questions after questions bombarded his mind. He was clueless as to why he had walked towards the mountain and spoke words that he could not comprehend. He saw parts of the mountain retreat to the ground, almost as if it was a door that had opened for Max. A breeze blew past him and it made him nauseous as it carried with him a horrible stench. Part of him was skeptical about the treasure in this mountain while another part was slightly happy that this could be the breakthrough he was desperately hoping for.

CHAPTER 7

"Yes!" Ashfaq exclaimed, breaking the silence and startling everyone. He was filled with joyous emotions and was glad he did not dispose of Max's group early on. He had witnessed the whole scene. The rumblings and the mysterious entrance took place right after Max placed his hand on the mountain. He compiled his findings and came to a conclusion that the reason the chair in the hut broke had something to do with Max. With this magnificent discovery, he could climb his way to the top and have people respect him as they should have. He would have access to the weapon that could consume the world. He would make those who had ridiculed him suffer and make the world beg on their knees. He quickly ordered his men to prepare for their entrance into the mountain. Flashlights were equipped on both their helmets and guns to provide as much lighting as possible. Entering the cave with as minimal light cover was stupid and Ashfaq was not one to enter with little preparation as possible.

He looked towards the kids and decided to allow them to follow his troops. He wanted Max to be there as there might be hidden devices that would require the presence of the boy. He needed to get close to the boy, to know what had happened in the hut. This was challenging for him as he was not a sociable kind and had been through multiple betrayals to never get close to another. For him, violence was always the answer. The strong will always rule over the week as that was what he had been taught ever since he was little. What use is connections in the world if someone stronger than you dictates your every move. He always believed that to survive in life, one must not trust anyone especially in a world where money had the power to influence. His men were there for him to utilise, for him to do the hard work instead. When he was glancing at the kids joking around and laughing, part of him yearned for a while. The rest was disgust as he wondered how they will feel when those closest to them backstabs them in their sleep. However, little does he care as once he had his hands on the weapon inside, he will test them against the kids for its effectiveness. It will be a good way to get rid of them.

Once his team was ready, they got into formation and entered the cave. The silence was eerie, making everyone on edge. Their concentration was at the peak condition. As they entered the cave, his men pan their lights around to get a better view of their surroundings. It was a spacious cave and whereby they felt as though they had stepped into another dimension. The walls towards his left took his attention. He instructed two of his men to light the area. It was interesting as the walls looked as though it was being dug. He walked towards the scattered skeletons located near the wall to inspect further. It was strange looking at the pieces of skeletons as he picked one up. It was a part of the hand which interested him the most as he focuses on the fingers. The fingers contained many scratches on the tip which led to him thinking maybe there was a connection between these skeletons and the hole in the wall. The hole was quite deep and a little more would have managed to dig through leading to the outside. To find the answers, they need to delve in deeper into the mountains.

As they walked in deeper into the mountains, the number of skeletons kept piling up. The question that was in everyone's mind was what could have happened deep inside the mountains. The lights they prepared were not enough to uncover the walkway. The darkness kept creeping up on them, trying to gobble them without the protection of the lights. He looked back and saw that the glowsticks they placed were still trying their hardest to light the walkway. They had travelled quite a distance but yet to make any improvements. Darkness was everywhere, seemingly trying to confuse them into walking into the abyss. He checked his watch to see how long they had been walking and saw that it had already been an hour. Furthermore, he was confused as to the reason there seems to be a lack of light source. Even in ancient times, the people would resort to torches to survive the darkness. However, he saw no such things even on the walls. How did people manage to maneuver in the darkness without the aid of the light. He felt this eerie feeling down his neck, as though someone was watching him. It was putting him on high alert and he felt uncomfortable with the lack of vision. The feelings intensified the further they walked in.

A few more hours of walking, the walkway opened up to a huge open space. Though with little light, they estimated the space to be as big as a football field. This was disturbing to Ashfaq as open spaces are ideal for traps that could hinder their progress. He then instructed the team to move to the centre of the open space. There was a possibility that the treasure would be there waiting for them to find it. Just as they were walking, one of his men shouted. The man continued to light towards the darkness and told Asfaq that he saw a shadow when he was lighting the area. Ashfaq instructed them to not fire upon any sign of contact. Firstly, it was to preserve the limited ammo that they had. The next was communication with any sort of contact would be ideal as it would hasten the process of finding the treasure. Hence it was imperative that they obtain any clues to uncover not only what happened here but also what lies hidden in this mountain.

Moments later, another one of his guards had claimed similar to the first. Panic and fear had started to run in the group. His men, despite undergoing heavy and intense training, were not equipped to counter this kind of situation. He instructed his men to calm down and to group into a circle formation with the kids in the centre. This was because they had no means of protection and Ashfaq would not like them to perish before he had completely utilised them. With this formation, they would have all angles covered, leaving no blind spots for the 'enemy' to take advantage of. They inched step by step, with the centre of the space as their objective. As soon as they reached the centre, he showed a hint of relief followed by shock as he saw what was waiting for them. Stood there were three figures that looked human but had different features. The three of them wore torn up tunics, barely able to cover any parts of their body. Their hairs were long almost like a lion's mane. One of them was a female due to the distinguishable feature that she had. The men were muscular in size, and he could barely make out the numerous scars they had on their body. Furthermore, these were different kinds of humans as they had large canine teeth. They looked ferocious, giving off a heavy aura. Ashfaq knew they were scanning his group, seemingly trying to find something. Then, the guy in the middle of the trio stepped forward. The moment he stepped forward, Ashfaq felt a heavy weight push down on him. He could hardly breathe or to continue standing. It took him his entire strength to struggle to gain control of his body. He was profusely sweating and was breathing heavily. He tried to look towards his group and saw that most of his men were kneeling on one knee, barely able to stand. Max's group was not faring well as the four of them were already on the floor, each gasping for breath. It seemed the bloodlust coming from the three were domineering to their group. However, Max was shockingly unaffected by the bloodlust as he tried to help his friends. It looked like the three were not in for any kind of conversation as they continued glaring, the aura oppressing them making them unable to move.

Suddenly, he heard his men shouting and panicking. They had claimed that two of their guys had vanished. He looked at the men and moments before he turned back, he saw it happen. One of his men was yanked into the darkness. It was done at a speed where it was surreal. He was too late to realize it as they had already walked into a trap. It was then that he decided that the other side was unfriendly and wanted to annihilate them hence he hastily ordered his men to open fire while retreating. He needs them to regroup and gather his thoughts and think about countermeasures. It was a one sided battle as they did not manage to land a single shot. It did not matter to him as their priority now was to get out of the cave and have the cover of sunlight. Fighting in the dark was disadvantageous for them as their enemies seemed to be accustomed to fighting in the dark. They desperately fought trying to reach the exit as it was challenging to find their indicators amidst the flashing gunfire. Once they saw the light from the exit, they felt reinvigorated and dashed straight for the exit. They were clinging on to the hope that the chase would stop once they did manage to escape. Eventually, after much running and gunning, they managed to bathe in sunlight. Their fear made them look back towards the entrance to check whether their foe was still hot on their tail. Emotions of relief took over their faces to see that there was nothing behind them, that they could take a breather from the horrifying chase.

‘Those people were out to kill us. Why were they out to kill us?’ Ashfaq thought and asked himself. Several things bothered him about their encounter. They were abnormally fast and strong, chasing them without stop and they disregarded the threat of the bullets as if it could not touch them. After that ordeal, he knew that they were confident in their speed, plus the ability to survive in the dark would make them the perfect assassins. If he could control them, there would be no one in this world who is safe, making him the most powerful man. For now, he should take in one step at a time and figure out how to capture those humans. Just as he decided to cordon off the entrance, one of the men approached him and told him that the kids had gone missing. Clicking his tongue at the misfortune, he shouted at his men to hasten the cordoning of the area to vent his anger.

CHAPTER 8

Max looked back to see whether Ashfaq's men were chasing him. After they had left the cave, Max immediately led his friends to retreat further back to escape from both Ashfaq and whatever that was inside the cave. He was surprised that the cave consists of people that probably had lived for so long. Despite the dark surroundings, Max could see that they were wearing torn clothings, barely covered. The three people just stood there, watching them as if inspecting who had entered their cave. Then it happened in an instant. One of the gunmen was dragged away followed by another a few moments later. Everything was blurry and the next thing he knew was they were running at their top speed from people they had just met. He did not realize that they had entered so deep and that the run back would be so excruciating.

They retreated further back, each of them exerting their last bit of energy to gain distance from the cave. It was a horrifying experience but also an eye-opener. It turned out at least one of the ancient civilizations does exist in the modern world. Max and their group found an ideal location to rest. A place that was far from the cave and one that is a walking distance to a river. Water is crucial to them as their water supply was running low and they needed to resupply themselves to last throughout the day. It was fortunate that Jane had seen the river which they could have missed. They made sure that no one was following them and had mixed up their trails to confuse any pursuers. Once they had settled down, they sat down to discuss their next actions. Jane shrieked when she looked at Max. They followed her line of sight and saw the reason why she had reacted. It turned out that Max's arm was bleeding. When he saw the injury, the pain reeled in and Max winced in pain. The adrenaline's effect had already subsided and now he was feeling the brunt impact of the pain. Wilhem crouched beside him and began to tend to the wound. When the wound was washed, it looked like Max was scratched on his arm. The scratch was abnormal as it was from his shoulder to his elbow. Max could not recall when it had happened as they were rushing away. Once the bandage was wrapped around his arm, they decided to stall the discussion to allow them to clear their mind from making any rash decisions. They made a small campfire as it was getting dark. This was their very first campfire and it did not spark any feelings of excitement. The mood was getting sour and it did not sit well with Max. Just as he was about to start a conversation, Jane and Haley had already begun talking.

"We saw them." Jane said, while covering her face. "There were two other people in there and they took the two gunmen."

Haley nodded and put an arm around her to comfort her.

The guys were shocked at this revelation. That meant that the three who stood there were just a trap to lure them in while the other two would flank and attack them from the side. They thought the three were there to converse with them but how wrong they were. They were the target.

Wilhem then walked towards his backpack and took out a skull. Max recognised the skull that was shown to him when they were at the village.

"Remember this. I took this skull with me as I wanted to study more on the biology of the people who had lived here. It took me the whole trip in the car to analyze and to put both puzzles together, I found something. Now, if you could take a look here." Wilhem said and then pointed to different parts of the skull. "These were not any normal marks, these were bite marks. Preferable scraping off any last bit of flesh they could off this skull. We all had a brief glance at whatever was in the cave and if what I saw was accurate, they had canine teeth. From the distance apart the canine teeth were from each other, I would say that they were the ones responsible for these marks."

The girls gasped while the guys could only look at Wilheim in disbelief. If what he had deduced is true, then the culprits were actually hunting them in the cave. Even with guns, they were able to outrun the trajectory and were hot on their tail. Max feared their future on the island and thought maybe it was time they depart from this island. The cave was supposed to be the barrier to keep whatever that was inside.

His hand suddenly felt like it was burning and the next thing he knew, he was alone in darkness. He turned around in panic, trying to find his friends. However hard he tried to call out, there was no response. From the distance, he could faintly hear footsteps. Approaching him at a calm pace, the figure stopped within a few metres from Max. Max could barely make out his face as there was a hood covering his head. He tried reaching for his phone to shed some light unto the figure but he could not find his phone. He tried to back away from the figure, but his legs felt like bricks and despite him trying his best to move, it was for naught.

"Peace be upon you, Max." the hooded figure began, his voice was smooth and surprisingly calming. Max was alarmed the figure knew his name considering he only just met him. A pair of questions lie on the tip of his tongue.

"Y...You s...speak English? How d..do you know my name?" Max desperately tried to keep his cool and asked.

"I know all there is to you ever since you touched my chair Max. My name is Al-Khail, ruler of the land here but now just a lost memory and I reside in your consciousness. I know this may sound shocking to you but we need to talk, Max." Al-Khail said. He then waved his hand, giving light to his surroundings. He sat at one of the two chairs and table which had appeared out of nowhere and motioned for Max to sit in front of him. Max looked at his surroundings once again to check whether he can escape from the person in front of him.

"In this space, there is only you and me. It is a futile effort Max. You cannot run from your own mind, Max. You can try though but it will be pointless. Plus, I know all the thoughts that reside in your mind too." Al-Khail said, smiling at him.

"What do you want from me?" Max asked, feeling dejected, reluctantly sitting on the chair. He was baffled at this revelation.

His mind was spinning and he needed answers. His thoughts went back to the chair which was the cause of everything that had happened to him, from his hands burning to meeting this strange man in front of him. As he had no escape route, he had to follow what was required of him to ensure his safety.

"Do not worry, my friend. Even though there is a time limit here, I will answer as best as I can for any of your questions. I will not hurt you as we will need each other to stop a massacre from happening in your time." Al-Khail said, looking at him before gazing into the abyss as if longing for something. "Before we begin, please listen to what had happened to the land and my people here years ago. We were a peaceful tribe, living in bliss and harmony. Color filled our lives and we were content with what we had..."

CHAPTER 9

Al-Khail left his room and looked at his wife and son in the kitchen, both attempting and challenging each other to cook their meals for dinner. With the help of a little magic, plates with ingredients and pans were flying everywhere. They were having fun and helping each other, laughter filling the house. He was happy with his life. Figuring that it would take awhile for them to finish, he went outside to visit the village and check how they were faring. He loves to talk to his people, to care for them regardless if it was his responsibilities as a king. He walked around the village, talking to his old friends and helping the villagers do their tasks. It gave him a sense of fulfilment that was indescribable.

He decided to head towards the meeting hall where all the discussions about the villages take place. There were loads of work to be done to improve on the conditions of the village. He had hoped to make the village a place where his son could rule with little to no problems. Along the way, he took in the breathtaking sights of the mountain view. It was surreal no matter how many times he saw it. The mountain that was the source of their magic. It was unbelievable when they first came to the island and found that there was something strange. Who knew that on this land, they would be able to conjure fire out of nowhere or to even catch fishes without even using the nets. Even though magic could be used to solve almost every single issue in the village, he would always emphasize to his people to never rely on it too much as it would only be a burden in the future. He feared the magic that the mountain produces would dry up and that would lead into unwanted circumstances.

Without realising, he had reached the front entrance of the meeting hall. He placed all those thoughts behind and entered the hall with a calm state of mind. He hoped today would be like any other day as he was hoping to taste the delicious dinner waiting for him. He shook his head and proceeded to sit on his chair located in the middle of the room. There were a few of his friends already seated and before long, the room was packed and ready for discussion. For the first few hours, the meeting was going relatively well. Knowing that the meeting was going to end soon, he sat on the edge of the chair, preparing to dash home to his lovely family. One of the elders stood up and kneeled before Al-Khair, bringing his attention back to the meeting hall. He assumed that the elder was from the other village as he could not recognize the older man.

"Respected elder, please stand up. There is no need for such things here." Al-Khair rushed to the elder and helped him stand. "What is the problem, respected elder?"

The elder leaned on to him and cried. It took him a while to gather his senses but Al-Khair did not mind as it looked like the elder had been through so much pain. Although he was uncomfortable with people breaking down, he wanted the elder to explain his situation with a clear mind. He tore part of his tunic and gave it to the elder to wipe his tears as there were no linen within reach. He conjured up a chair for the elder to sit on, brought his own chair to sit near the elder and waited calmly for the elder to continue his story.

The elder timidly took the torn leather and sat down with much haste, most probably feeling guilty having cried and making the king wait for him. He started to describe what had happened and the contents shocked the members in the room. The elder, Salaywal, was from a fishing village located on the other side of the island. They were a peaceful village that had cooperated with them for generations.

The elder mentioned several days before, other tribes had come from the seas in large boats. They were all wearing black tunics, some had menacing tattoos while the others wore helmets made from animal skulls, they were standing on the edge of their boats with each eager to step foot on the shore. One of the villagers was standing on the shore, to serve as a representative of the village responsible for welcoming the other party and to establish communications. Before he could react, one of the boatmen jumped down and hacked his axe unto the unsuspecting villager. It took the villagers a while before they realised what was happening and this drove the villagers into a state of panic. Some of them were still stunned at what had just happened as it was surreal to watch one of their own get killed before their very eyes. This was the first time that they had faced any sort of violence and the only thing on their mind now was their survival. Furthermore, the way the other tribe moved was extraordinary as they were moving swiftly and coordinated. They locked on to their targets and striked without hesitation.

The villagers were slaughtered mercilessly and devoured leaving no women and children safe from their onslaught. The survivors attempted to run for their lives, each scattering in different directions into the jungle, hoping that the forest would be able to shield or at least hide them from the attack. The elder wept as he said that even the defenseless were unsafe from those savages. They could not defend themselves as it occured instantly and before long, most of their people were annihilated, dismembered parts everywhere. Salaywal could vaguely remember that near the back of the tribe, they were frantically collecting the dismembered parts and placing it in their baskets. They then stacked the buckets as if stocking them to use for later. Some of them were fighting and gnawing with each other, defending their trophies and food. The elder and his son ran as fast as they could to get help. Perhaps Salaywal wished that he could seek revenge on these dwellers that massacred his family. Their run seemed endless, their legs were getting sore but they knew that if they were to take a moment to rest, they would have to fight a losing battle against those beasts. They were exhausted and were dying of thirst, their body begging them to take a breather, the pain getting more excruciating every step forward. Night was coming soon and they were at an impasse. They could either continue running through the night to reach the other village or they could find a secluded place to rest through the night. This would be a critical moment as the longer they take, the risk of the other village getting massacred increases. They could make a beeline for the other village but Salaywal knew his body could not make it.

Hence, he turned towards his son and asked him to go on ahead.

"No Dad. I would not leave you here." His son whispered, annoyance and anger could be felt in his tone.

They were the only survivors of the village, Salaywal did not want to weigh down his son and explained to him that it was imperative they warn the other village as they did not want the same thing to happen to them. Salaywal felt that his son had a better chance at survival alone than together with him. The most he could do now was to stall the progress of the invaders. As they were both insisting on their own plans, it was already dark and filled with silence. They knew it was impossible to continue to argue further hence decided to find a place to rest for the day as going forward without light would only confuse them further.

Try as he might, Salaywal could not sleep. Flashbacks of what had happened haunted him. Images of his wife, his daughters and his family being torn apart and devoured fueled his rage. Many regrets filled his mind. He clenched his teeth at his weakness and cried. There was nothing that could bring them back. He turned on his sides and looked at his son. His heart was heavy as he looked at his son, how his son had his wife's features. That was when he had decided to lead his son to safety at the cost of his own. No more of his family members should be sacrificed to the invaders. He shall attempt to slow them down, perhaps bringing a few along with him. Having resolved his heart and mind, he slowly drifted off to sleep.

He woke up to a new surrounding, unfamiliar with what was before his eyes. He rubbed his eyes a few more times before he could make out the village before him. He stood up in a flash and frantically looked around for his son. He asked the villagers surrounding him only to find out that he was left there by the figure who dashed back into the forest. His knees gave way and started to cry knowing that he may never see his son again. He felt lost and did not know what else to do. Took him awhile before he resolved himself and asked for directions before heading towards the village chief's location to warn them of the coming danger. He would fulfil this duty of sharing the enemies weakness before resting to join his family.

Upon hearing what Salaywal had to say, the meeting room was void of any noise. No one could believe what they were hearing. Some were sceptical of the elder's story as it did not make any sense to them. It was baffling that a whole fishing village was decimated in a short period of time. Without listening more to the other people in the room, Al-Khair decided to take action and instructed to prepare defences for the invaders. There was no harm if Salaywal was false. This would help prepare them for any future altercations with the other villages. However, if Salaywal was telling the truth, he would do anything to protect his family and preparing the defences was paramount for their survival. Man-eating people had come to their island looking for food and they were on the menu.

The whole village was in a frenzy. People were dashing everywhere to prepare themselves for an invasion that might or might not come. Men were dashing from the forest to the village, gathering wood and necessities for their defenses. Some of them were busy sharpening their swords and spears. Al-Khair also instructed his people to build necessary forts and trenches to better safeguard his village from the incoming attack. It was hectic but they efficiently constructed the defenses surrounding the village, leaving no sides uncovered. Once everything was set in place, Al-Khair allowed his people to spend the remaining quality time with their family. He was praying that it was not real and they could live on peacefully but his heart was saying otherwise. Something in him was yelling that their preparations were not enough. Looking at the village, he did not want to burden his people any longer. Hence, feeling that the defences were acceptable, he proceeded back to his house to meet his family. He could not wait to spend time with his family and to eat what they had prepared so tediously for him. He placed the unnecessary thoughts at the back of his head as he would not want to worry his family in case it ever showed on his face.

Al-Khair sat at his dining table with his family, enjoying their quality time together. He tried to fully enjoy his time with his family after the shocking news he had heard today. He needed to put the meeting that took place at the back of his head. He feared thinking any further would show on his face and would cause unnecessary worry. It opened his eyes to the current situation. They were too content with their lives that they took everything they had for granted.Despite him trying his best to fully enjoy the savoury food his wife and son had made, he could not fully enjoy it. His heart felt heavy as if something was weighing him down. He was gazing at the interactions of his family members when the image of Salaywal popped up in his head. He recollected the old man sobbing after he had told his story. Hearing how the other village was met with misfortune and their family members were brutally taken from them made him cherish his family and his people even more. He did not want to place himself in the Salaywal's shoes as he could not imagine the torture Salaywal must have felt. He wanted to stop the time, to abandon everything else and to live in the bliss moment that they were having. Alas every good thing must end as he saw their empty plates. Out of instinct, he glanced out the window and noticed the time. He hated himself for it as it brought him back to reality. It was time to go back to the meeting hall and to find out whether what the old man had said was really true. He kissed his wife and bid farewell to his family before setting off.

When he reached the meeting hall, it was surprisingly quiet. The moment he stepped into the hall, the intensity of the room hit him. It was a heavy aura and he could see not only the anxious faces, there were several faces that were exhausted in the meeting room. He could only assume that there had been a massive argument that took place before he had entered the room. The situation was stressful for him, giving him a headache. Just as they were about to discuss further on their next steps, the door banged open and a youth gaspingly ran in. The young boy looked terrified and was struggling to breathe after sprinting his best to where they were.

"They...They're here." The youth said in between gasps, trying to gain back his composure. This revelation set the whole room in chaos as they were desperately hoping otherwise. Their hopes were crushed, faces drained of color as reality hit them hard. Some began wailing and crying desperately, their tears streaming down their faces while dropping to their knees. Al-Khaid saw some of the elders struggling to get back to their feet, while some others were on their backs against the walls saying repeatedly that they had given up. Without waiting any further for the tension to rise, he stood up and demanded attention. He quickly gave his orders, making sure that their families safety was a priority. Then, he proceeded to instruct the elders to fall back with the rest while he brought the able-bodied men to confront the invaders.

He stood in front of his men, in front of their village entrance. Between them and the forest lie a trench that was dug up to prepare for this moment. He had hoped that the trench would at least slow the invaders down and allow him and his men to thin out their numbers. He was concerned when he saw the people that he would be up against. They were as what the old man had said. Mighty warriors and the aura they gave was heavy. They look deadly and hungry, some of them had licked their lips upon looking at the villagers.

Al-Khaid looked solemn when Max took a glance. Max could feel the pain in Al-Khaid's voice when hearing the other's tale. Even after so many years had passed by, it still impacted heavily on Al-Khaid and this had shown his love for his people. Al-Khaid stopped talking and looked at a certain direction, as if he had sensed something.

"It appears we have to cut the story short Max. They have come for you, i can feel their anger and hunger."Al-Khaid told him. "Be careful Max. Those savages are ruthless and will destroy anything in its path. Let us meet again sometime." Al-Khaid continued before snapping his fingers sending Max away from the place.

Max opened his eyes to see the campfire along with his friends. Heeding his mysterious companion's advice, he extinguished the campfire and quickly instructed his friends to start moving. They left the place hastily, without much questions. While retreating to find a safer place, they made sure to not leave any trail by going through several routes before proceeding to hopefully confuse their pursuers.

CHAPTER 10

The day felt longer than usual and fatigue had replaced the adrenaline, their bodies screaming for attention demanding the rest that they needed. It dawned upon them that the island was much bigger than it seemed. Without any compass and map, they were running in a straight direction, hoping that they would eventually stumble upon the village or the pier. The situation was not getting better as it was soon going to be dark and they had not found any suitable place to make camp. Max was getting more nervous by the second. The vision that was shared to him by Al-Khaid was so real and it felt like he was witnessing it in person. He hoped that there would be another chance to talk to Al-Khaid again to find out more what really happened on the island. What used to be a land of prosperous people turned into a land devoid of people. A mountain filled with humans with inhuman abilities was unheard of. Everytime he thought back to their encounter in the mountains sent shivers down his spine.

They seemed to have been running for hours until they had finally stumbled upon a cave. Though it might have blocked off any chance of escape, they desperately needed to rest. They were all heavily panting, exerting every little effort they could muster to carry on running. Without thinking much longer, Max decided to lead them inside the cave for the night. It was imperative that they rest and recuperate to gain back their energy to escape. He hoped deep inside that Ashfaq and his men were able to eliminate the inhabitants of the cave if not at least stall them so that Max and his friends could leave the island. It was harsh but Max had to put the safety of his friends first and he knew that they would be of little help to Ashfaq. Max could not believe his luck this few days. What had started to be a peaceful expedition had become a life or death situation. Furthermore, he had his friends' lives on his hands and that made him panic more. A wrong move at any point of time could endanger their lives which could even result in their death. The further he thought about the negative consequences, the greater his fear. He looked towards his friends, thinking of any solution for them to escape the ordeal that they are in. Never in their lives had they come across any situation like this. He was never prepared for this outcome. He wanted to wake up any moment and pass off these few days as a nightmare. His mother would wake him up at any moment and comfort him in her arms. He looked towards the sky and was starting to tear, his memory of his mom flashing constantly in his mind. He prayed for the chance to give his mother a hug and to keep telling her everything was fine. Since it was getting dark, Max led his friends to camp in the cave as it was much safer compared to sleeping out in the open where danger lurks at every angle. Each of them was relieved that they finally managed to give their bodies and mind a rest. It was taxing crucially on their well-being. They needed answers and looked towards Max as he would usually have all the answers. The moment their gazes landed upon Max, they were taken aback. Max looked distraught, his face bare of color. His knees kept constantly tapping, deep in thought. They left him alone for a while as it would only worsen the situation otherwise. The dark and still night did nothing to lighten the grim situation. Each of them hardly could get any sleep. It was ironic given the exhaustion they felt. Twist and turn did each of them try, trying to find the ideal position to get that sleep no matter how little. Eventually, they managed to get the sleep they desperately needed.

Max woke up to the lights from the entrance of the cave. It was already half past eleven, they had overslept and might possibly lose the advantage that they had the night before. On the other hand, his friends were all drained from the travel yesterday so it would not matter that much if they were to delay their departure. His brain was groggy and he could not properly form any thoughts. He took a sip out of a bottle of water hc took out from his backpack. His body rejoiced coolly when the water entered his body. Though it was not as refreshing as he had hoped, it was at least something. He looked outside the cave, though the scenery was mesmerising, there was no time to take in the scenery as he had to decide the direction they would go next. To prevent their morale dropping even further and raising needless panic, he decided to not tell them the fact that they were lost. He would not want to crush their hopes and not misplace their trust on him. He took out a piece of paper and began sketching. He was quite vexed with himself for not doing this much earlier. It could have saved them plenty of time.

Once his friends had all woke up and preparations were complete, they departed to find their yacht as everyone wanted to get away from the island and go back home. As they were just about to leave the cave, they heard the rustling noises nearby. They halted in their tracks and began to move carefully. It was never a good sign when leaves were rustling unnaturally. They treaded carefully, using the trees to hopefully cover them as they moved along. Max felt a tug on his sleeves and saw Haley holding it with a frightened expression. Her fingers trembled as they moved to point towards a certain direction. Seeing Haley tremble, Max slowly turned towards the direction. There he clearly saw them. This was their second encounter yet they felt as if they had seen it for the first time. This time, they are able to see clearly what was inside the caves due to the light and what they saw was not something they would want to see ever again. Two human-like figures, standing next to each other, glaring at them. It looked like they were observing him and his friends. Max looked at them and from their features appeared to be two males standing with their arms crossed. One of them had a scar along his face, his body rugged muscular as if he had played rugby his whole life. The other was skinny to the point where his bones could clearly be seen. He was missing one of his eyes, which in turn sickened Max and his group as whenever he opened his missing eye, there seemed to be hollow and nothing inside. The other guy made no attempt to hide his empty eye socket and kept smiling wickedly. This confrontation was making Max shiver as at the moment, they were at the other party's mercy. They had no way to escape should the other party act. They were staring at each other for some time before one of them started conversing with the other. Max was actively sweeping through the location, trying to find him and his friends a way out of the intense situation. He motioned for his friends to retreat slowly, taking step by step and not alerting them of their intentions. What happened next was out of their expectations. The duo were smiling at each other, took a glance at Max and his friends before vanishing away.

'They left...just like that?' Max pondered as he found it weird that they would leave like they did. He was bewildered by what had happened as they could have been killed if the other party felt like it. Snapping out of the many speculations in their heads, they carried their stuff and proceeded to run back. For what seemed like hours, Max felt that they were walking in circles. There seemed to be no exit. Every few minutes, he would glance at their rear as he felt the gaze of someone. It felt as though someone was stalking them, watching their every move. It was an uncomfortable feeling which made him fasten the pace of their group. He would not want another confrontation with those hunters again. Even guns did not manage to slow those ancient people down.

The sight of the sea brought the anticipated relief to them. They will be able to sail back home and possibly forget the incident entirely, treating it like it did not exist. The girls, clinging to the hope of reaching the boat, started beelining towards the shore. The guys on the other hand, decided to walk instead to conserve whatever energy they had left. One of the girls fell to her knees and started crying and thrashing the sand about. The guys hurriedly went to their side and saw the cause. Their hopes were utterly shattered. There were no piers in sight, just a plain beach and the wide open sea. The guys, not wanting to give up hope, ran towards each direction, hoping for a glimpse of the pier to bring back as good news to raise their morale. The beach seemed to stretch for miles no matter how much they ran. The pier was nowhere to be seen.

'This.. This..' Max struggled to form words, with his emotions running wild. 'Got to run a bit more. Maybe the pier is just around the corner.' He ran for miles yet there seems to be no breakthrough in his search for hope. The hope for going home seemed to be diminishing every mile he ran. He continuously ran, gathering as much energy as he could to fuel his legs, it was imperative that he kept on as he knew if he were to stop to take a short breather, he would lose his chance and would give up. Eventually, his legs gave way and he landed on the grainy sand. Gasping for breath and looking around the beach for the pier, he was utterly disappointed and his hopes shattered as there was not even a glimpse of the pier. How he wished that he could pretend all of this had never happened and that they would still be at their houses living their normal lives.

He walked back to where his friends were, his back slouched forward. Each step felt heavier and the fear he felt was much greater compared to before. He truly did not wish to face his friends now and to tell them that there was no hope of getting off the island. He dragged his feet, trying to delay as much as he could from meeting his friends. When he saw their silhouettes from a distance, his heart clenched and the moment he feared was near. The moment they caught sight of him, they surrounded and bombarded him with questions, faces filled with anticipation of going home. Max suddenly felt dizzy, his brain was trying to keep up with the questions whilst also trying to figure out a way to break down the bad news subtly. Max signalled for them to sit down while he tried his best to muster whatever courage he could to face his friends.

As soon as he had explained their situations, some began to cry while the others stood and began walking in different directions, probably trying to clear their heads. Silence fell upon them, each with their own thoughts. Max wanted to ease the situation, to lighten the mood but to no avail. Deep down, he blamed himself for their predicament. If he was not adamant influencing them to embark with him on this journey, they would not be where they were now. Darkness crept up slowly surrounding them as night approached. His head was dizzy, mind in turmoil unable to properly form even a single sentence in his head. His heart was heavy and he had difficulty breathing.

"You'll only burden them more if you stay with them. They are better off without you. They would not be in this mess if not for you."

He could barely sleep as the day kept replaying in his mind. The disappointed gazes by his friends' faces weighed down his heart. He had to do something. The only way out of this island would be to find their boat, or in worst scenarios to find some sort of transportation. He packed his back and crept silently towards the forest. He needed to be stealthy to avoid waking his friends up. Once he knew he was within a few metres away from his friends, he ran deeper into the jungle disregarding any noise he made. For now, he had to quickly find a shelter to pass the night. His desperation increased as time passed by. A shelter was very rare in the forest. There seemed to be nowhere suitable for him to spend the night. In the end, he gave up and decided to climb a tree to sleep on one of the branches. He assumed it would be at least safer compared to sleeping on the ground in the open. The cons of sleeping on the ground greatly encouraged him to decide on the branch as his resting place. The climb was challenging as he was not the athletic type. It drained him and left his arms sore. There were bruises on his fingers and it hurts. For someone who abhors pain, pain seemed to be of a frequent occurrence ever since he came to this island. Once he had found a suitable branch, he tied himself to the trunk of the tree so that there would not be any unfortunate accident during his sleep. He sighed to himself before looking towards the distance as he thought about his mother and his friends. All the things left unsaid to his mother brought a tear to his eyes. Just as he was about to sleep, he heard rustling of the leaves below. Hugging his legs as tightly as he can, he forced himself to be as quiet as he could. With his vision impaired due to the eerie darkness, he prayed that whatever made the rustles would just pass by and not notice him up on that branch. He shut his eyes tight, thinking that it would go away soon. The rustles grew louder by the minute.

Then, he heard them. They were talking to each other. It was in a language that was unknown to him. From the tone of their voices, it sounded as if they were arguing with each other. It seemed as though they were intent on staying there. Max was desperately hoping that they would leave. Despite his hopes, these foreign beings seemed keen on staying there. To his dismay, they decided to light a fire right below his tree. They kept on talking to each other, sometimes screaming. At one point, Max even heard them brawling with one other before laughing the next second. He had observed that these individuals were keen on violence as their brawling had managed to injure all of them yet they were able to shrug it off as if nothing had happened. The longer Max observed them, the weirder he got as it looked like these individuals were not exhausted at all. Max could not sleep as his adrenaline was on the high and it was close to impossible to take a nap with killers dwelling right beneath him. Max was exhausted due to the lack of sleep. They would not leave and it looked like they did not depend on sleep as their energy levels did not seem to be depleted. They had finally left the place after so long, making Max sigh in relief.

CHAPTER 11

He woke up, his eyes groggy, gaining focus by the minute. Even though the sleep had not been satisfactory, he was relieved that he still managed to get at least some sleep in. He thought about his priorities and the first one was to find Ashfaque or at least his fire powers. Max knows that he could not resolve this peacefully as he had discerned the violent nature of those beings. They loved to fight and kill as he saw them sink their teeth into live animals killing them instantly. That gore method of killing was horrendous and Max threw up thinking about it again. What was different about them is that they did not skin the animals nor do they dry them of their blood. They seemed to enjoy drinking the blood of their victims. The fear that these beings emitted was terribly immense that could be felt by him high up in the tree.

Max decided against provoking them as another reason was to find out more about what they were facing against. He needed to find out what were their weaknesses so that they could at least mount a counter-attack against these foes. He knew that defeating these foes was paramount for their escape away from this island. The next issue was they were headed towards his friends and he could not place them in danger after all they had been through. Hoping he could find Ashfaque, he began running through the forest back to the cave as that would be a good starting point for him. He tried to remember the route they had taken, trying to put bits and pieces of his memories together. It seemed like hours before he felt that he had finally reached the entrance to the cave once again. He bent over, his hands on his knees, gasping for air. Every fibre of his body burning again. His head had started to hurt, and his eyes were losing focus. He forced himself to keep moving and find Ashfaque's team. However, as his vision started to clear, he was shocked to see what was before him. The ground was painted red and there were pieces of flesh everywhere. The air was filled with a pungent smell that hit him straight away, causing him to almost puke. He had to cover his nose to navigate through and as he walked forward, his hope began to diminish. It seemed that it was a one sided battle as he could barely see the vests that were lying on the ground. As he picked up one of the vests, he found out that the vest was torn in half. He noticed that the vest did not seem like it was cut clean through as he could see marks along the edges of the vest. He kept looking around for survivors but as time passed by, he only managed to find several more corpses from Ashfaque's team.

"Inside." Max heard the voice inside his head and looked towards the entrance of the cave. He was hesitant about going into the cave as fear from what had previously happened had taken over him. He paced in front of the entrance, trying to steel himself and gather himself to enter the cave. He took a few more deep breaths before he picked up his pace and entered the cave. Any slower and he feared that he would turn around and it would all be over for him and his friends. As he went deeper and deeper into the cave, he was starting to have second thoughts. He could barely see through the dark and his flashlight was doing little to improve the situation. He stuck himself close to the wall so that he would not aimlessly wander through the cave. As he knew that there would be a huge opening later on, it was best to hug the walls of the cave as it could help him navigate through the large cave. How he wished the voice in his head would talk to him right now as the silence was killing him. Every step he took, he would glance in all directions. Regardless of whether he could see or not, it made him slightly safer to check his surroundings for any potential danger.

Just as he was about to reach the center of the cave, he was shoved down and felt a hand around his throat. He was stunned by the sudden lights and it took him awhile for him to regain his vision. He felt an object pressed on his forehead before he realised that whoever had taken him down had pressed a gun on his forehead. He did not move as he was afraid that if he were to retaliate now, he would be shot in this cave. He then heard a few men chattering among themselves. He recognised some of the voices to be the men of Ashfaq's team.

"What are you doing here boy? I should kill you right now and feed you to whatever those things are." A deep, exhausted voice sounded. "That way, at least we could observe and determine just what those beings were."

Upon hearing the voice, Max found the voice was familiar

and squinted his eyes a couple of times before noticing that it belonged to Ashfaq who was holding him at gunpoint. He managed to see their weary faces and their battered up clothes. They had barely managed to survive the confrontation with those things. Ashfaq then put away his gun before slumping to the ground and sighed.

"Part of me should be thankful that you were the one who entered the cave, kid. If those things enter again, this place could very well be our graveyards." Ashfaq continued. "Why'd you come in alone without your friends?" He proceeded to ask after finding out that Max had ventured in alone.

Max turned away from Ashfaq to hide his emotion. He did not want to disclose any unnecessary information to Ashfaq.

"We need to take down whatever those things are." He said, trying to shift their attention to the main issue that they were facing. He could not tell them that he did not want to bring any harm to his friends. This would mean that he would rather sacrifice Ashfaq's team. If the other party were to know his true intention, there would be no common grounds for negotiation. He quickly stood up and dusted off the dust from his clothes. He looked over the condition of Ashfaq and his team and saw that they were not doing so well. It was a gruesome sight as some of them had lost part of their limbs while the rest were looking exhausted and rough around the edges. Even though he knew his value was not comparable to the other, he figured he would at least be helpful in certain areas of the battle that hopefully would take place. He would be devastated if Ashfaq decides to retreat away from the island rather than confronting those anomalies. This would then ruin his plans on securing his friends' safety and survival.

Without dwelling on the matter of Max's friends, Ashfaq sighed and turned around. Not wanting to press further on an unimportant subject, he simply nodded and moved on. However, he was at a loss too at how to win an encounter with whatever that was outside. There was no means of survival and his calculation in his head had deduced that their probability of surviving their next clash is less than favourable. He knew that these violent creatures would be difficult to control yet if someone does manage to, they will hold power over the world. As enticing as that sounds, he had to figure out a way to neutralise them and perhaps a way to train them so that they will obey his every command. That will require a lot of effort and manpower, those he was severely lacking. Furthermore, it was better to kill them rather than letting them survive as he feared the consequences should they fall in enemy hands. Surely his superiors' will understand why he had to do what he did. He attempted to formulate a plan to kill whatever those things are yet none came to mind. They were simply outmatched in every aspect. Do they even have any chance to begin with? Without minding much, he began looking for Max to try and get a fresh perspective on their plan however futile it may be. He listened to what Max had to say, the history and how those things came to this island. Ashfaq did not know how to process the information. These beings are more fearsome than he had imagined. To be able to survive for this long can only be called legends. How there were little records of them in the history books are a wonder in itself. There was only a single piece of good news that could have been taken away from their conversation; the enemies numbers had dwindled down to a few of them left.

He slumped backwards against the wall, trying to regain any kind of composure he could muster after hearing the devastating news was a challenge in itself. Perhaps with the use of bigger weapons and vehicles could they stand a chance to combat those brutes. The bigger issue was he could not find any way to contact the outside world. Their satellite phones were not working and all their communication devices had been short-circuited by the massive storm trying to reach the island. With their ammunition running low, it seemed as if their expedition here was meant to end in failure. Did those people know that this was going to happen? Ashfaq shouted out in anger, trying to clear his mind.

CHAPTER 12

Max felt the cold ground under his hands when he looked at how Ashfaq looked at him with contempt. Max detested that man, but for the sake of his friends, he had to be by his side to find a way to get rid of those humanoids or, in the worst of cases, take them away from his friends.

Ashfaq paced from side to side. He seemed to be highly concerned about the situation. He was looking at his men with complicated expressions, wondering if he could carry out his mission.

After a moment of silence, Ashfaq looked at Max and said. "You are lucky I did not kill you, child. Where is the rest of your crew?"

Max looked at him, and taking a breath, he said, "They left. The truth is I lost track of them. I don't know if they are dead or abandoned. I couldn't find the ship we got here on either."

Max did his best to sound forceful, but Ashfaq's eyes did not seem to give him respite. They studied him as if they could read his mind, and the pressure that Max felt made him sweat, suddenly in the distance, a roaring journey all over the island.

Ashfaq looked outside the cave, and with a resigned smile, he said, “I have no choice but to believe what you say. Trust me, I would like nothing more than to kill you, but I really need all the hands I can use!”

The boy stood up, and the soldiers looked at him as if he could give him some hope. Apparently, when they saw him open the cave the first time, they developed the belief that he was connected with those things in some way. That idea was not easy to shake out of those guys' minds.

Ashfaq approached, and with the same curiosity of the soldiers, he asked, “You know something about this island, don't you?”

Max looked at him. He had to be careful with the information he gave. Otherwise, he couldn't keep his friends safe, he replied as calmly as he could, “I know how those things got here! We got some manuscripts that explained it!”

Ashfaq looked at him, interested. It was as if his mind anticipated everything Max was going to say. At that time, he asked, “Let me guess, your friends took the manuscript, didn't they?”

Max had no choice but to nod at the devilish gaze of the military man.

“Your friends are real rats! Look at you? They leave you in this place to your own luck! Kid, you have to be ruthless to survive! It doesn’t matter if they say that you are a soulless person!" The military man said, as if reprimanding Max.

Max felt a deep offense with those words, but he knew that it was not the time to let himself be carried away by his instincts.

"Do you have any idea how to deal with those creatures?" Max asked carefully, while looking at Ashfaq.

The man saw him with a half-smile and approaching the exit of the cave, he said, "The same way we deal with all threats, with brute force!" At that moment, Ashfaq smiled and, looking at the boy again, said, "The truth is that the weapons we have at hand will not be able to face those bastards. They are extraordinarily fast and evil creatures. We need something more powerful!"

Max looked at him when Ashfaq turned again, took his rifle, and said with a wide smile, "This can shoot almost 60 rounds per minute and still not enough!" as he

"But in my primary camp, there are good weapons that we can use to destroy these disgusting creatures!" Ashfaq continued confidently.

Ashfaq repeated that he wanted to eliminate these threats, but that was not entirely true. While he hoped he could get to his main camp to gather the weapons he had brought, his intention was clearly different. However, he still had not managed to discover the weak point of those creatures, and without a doubt, he thought that Max was the connection for that.

The way the entrance to the cave had manifested in front

of him was clearly the sign that his presence had weight. Ashfaq was more than willing to use that advantage if it meant having to sacrifice all of his men.

However, allowing the young man to find out about that would be a mistake, his story still seemed illogical. He had said many things made no sense whatsoever, but he would let them pass for the moment.

Looking at the men, he said, "While here, we will be just cannon fodder! At first light, we will go into full gear towards the main camp!"

When he said that, the following words from him, although addressed to the whole group, seemed personal when looking directly into Max's eyes when he said, "There will only be one pace! Who can't keep it up, well prepare to be monster food!"

Max looked at him, and then all the men in the cave, at least ten well-armed men laughed, and all gave him mixed looks between fear and pity, but it was the feeling of reproach that Max had inside him.

He sat in the corner of the cave. He was determined not to fall asleep, he did not know exactly what time it would dawn, but he was sure that those soldiers would not wake him up. Without a doubt, things would get ugly, and he had to be prepared.

His mind traveled to his friends on the beach and stole with all his might that they were okay. His gaze alternated between the piece of sky that could be seen through the entrance to the cave and a drop that sounded every time it touched a pool of water inside.

The soldiers had directed powerful reflectors of light into the cave to ensure they were not caught off guard. Still, despite the power of these lamps, the darkness of the cave seemed to engulf everything.

His gaze was lost in the blackness when his eyes felt like someone was watching him, a creature seemed to be prowling further than the light allowed him to see, and Max watching that show was defeated by sleep and fell asleep.

Ashfaq looked apprehensively at the boy who was clearly falling asleep in the corner of the cave. His hand trembled as his revolver cried out to end the life of the little bastard. Still, his instinct was clear, that child would undoubtedly be the key, and only a fool would lose him that way, and if there was something that he was not, that was a fool.

While he was clearly observing him, his right hand reached the corner of the cave that he occupied and said, "Mister! Think we can get to the camp tomorrow!"

Ashfaq looked at Klivert. He was, without a doubt, his best soldier and the man he trusted the most. Smiling, he said, "Yes! We will arrive! But I need something more from you!"

Klivert looked at him curiously when Ashfaq said, "That brat's story doesn't seem entirely true. I don't know if they want to set a trap for us or if he thinks he is smart enough to gamble. In any case, we need to anticipate."

Klivert nodded as his eyes looked at Max, who breathed

calmly in the place where he had sat. Looking back at the commanding officer, he asked, “Do you want me to find his friends?”

Ashfaq smiled. He knew that his best man would understand the situation instantly and calmly, he said, “I would not ask this of anyone else. And if there was another way...”

“You don't have to justify yourself to me, sir,” Klivert said, interrupting the rehearsed apology Ashfaq was about to give him when he said, “An order is an order, and you can be sure I will carry it out!”

Ashfaq grinned before he said, “Perfect! Listen. Follow the trail he left to get here. Hopefully, he's just an idiot who broke away from his group but proceeds with caution, the creatures are loose, and we don't know what those kids are up to.”

Klivert took a firm stance and, giving a military salute, prepared to leave when Ashfaq said, “Take a radio. I will contact you when I need to know your progress or if there is a change of plans.”

Klivert nodded, took a radio, the rules team from him, and left the cave without a hint of doubt in his mind. He started walking briskly as he found the trail that Max had left. As he did so, he smiled. The boy hadn't even tried to cover his advance. As he advanced, he felt movement behind him, and raising his rifle, he pointed fearfully but saw nothing.

His nervousness was justified, but he needed to stay calm. Taking a deep breath, he resumed his way. At dawn, the soldiers in the cave stood up, and it was Ashfaq himself who, kicking one of Max's legs, made him get up.

The man looked at him in surprise, and seeing his smile, he heard him say, Get ready, kid! It's time to leave!"

***

CHAPTER 13

Klivert was walking behind the trail that Max had left. The boy's footprints were erratic and fearful. The decision to leave his friends had been hasty, which went completely against what he had said. Ashfaq was right. The boy was lying.

As he got to the beach, he could see how Max's footsteps led him back to a makeshift camp that they had made on the beach. When he reached that point, Klivert stopped and completely studied all the traces there.

"They were here! Until midnight! But something made them move!"

Looking around him, he saw the footprints of his companions. They weren't trying to hide the trail of him, and even someone like Max could follow them without a problem. Clearly, they had not left him. He had left them, but why?

Without knowing what the reason would be, Klivert followed the trail of Max's companions. The boys had taken the safest path and followed the beach in the hope of reaching the ship. Max had lied about everything, he could understand that he wanted to protect his friends, but those silly lies would make Ashfaq completely angry.

He started to follow the trail left by those boys when he felt a presence looking at his back. It was the second time he felt that and raising his weapon pointed towards the forest. Dawn was coming, but he still couldn't see what was hiding and was watching him.

He had thought it was his imagination, but clearly, it was not, someone was following him, and that made him nervous, looking in the direction of the forest he could not identify movement. With a deep breath he decided to follow the tracks that Max's friends had left.

When he found them, he could undoubtedly use them to get all the information they could from Max. Ashfaq was sure that the boy knew something else and was not sharing that information. Without a doubt finding those friends that he abandons could be a way of putting pressure on him.

But at that moment, a thought paralyzed him. What if this boy was heartless? Abandoning his friends to protect them was one thing, but what if he was just switching sides to increase his chances of survival.

He certainly did not seem like one of those terrible traitors who would sacrifice anyone for their own well-being. Still, if the war had taught him anything, it was that judging a person by their appearance was a terrible tactical error, not quite sure what to believe.

Klivert looked at the trail again and taking a deep breath

he said, “Whatever you're doing, Max will find out when I catch your friends.”

And with those words, the persecution began.

At a considerable distance, the trail Klivert was beginning to follow led to Max's friends, who were shuffling along with exhaustion. John tried to keep up the optimism, but his attempts were futile. All his friends were completely discouraged by the recent news, and Sam, who was looking at the sea, said what many of them had thought. Still, no one dared to say out loud.

“Do you think Max found the ship and left us here to die?”

John turned to reprimand him for that comment, but Sam's gaze showed him that in his heart that possibility grew. Still, it was impossible, how many years of friendship they had and how could he believe that about his friend, whoever left them surely had a great explanation.

But not a word came out of his mouth to defend him. While he was thinking of saying a voice that he really didn't expect him to hear, he raised Max's defense forcefully when Haley said, “Don't be stupid, Sam! Look.. He left all the supplies! He didn’t even take a flashlight! Does that seem to you like he left us to die?”

Sam lowered his head and clenched his fist. He couldn't believe what he had said, but he was seized with exhaustion, and his mind was in turmoil. John saw him and tried to get closer to offer him words of comfort when Wilhem, with more force than he intended, grabbed his forearm.

John saw it, but Wilhem, asking for silence, pointed towards the forest. Seeing in the direction that his friend was pointing, John looked at how a shadow moved slowly. They all held his breath, but John, making a sign, hurriedly told them to keep walking at that moment.

They did not know what that movement was or if it was directed at them, but without a doubt, they should hurry and leave that place. When he got up in the morning, the least he expected to happen was that his best friend had abandoned him. Dealing with that was bad enough, but dealing with the fact that now everyone was on an island full of cannibalistic monsters was still worse.

Walking at a steady pace, the beach came to a point where it collided with a hill. The hill was very high, and there was a cliff that overlooked the ocean at the top of it. As much as they want to stay on the beach, it would be impossible. The path must now be diverted.

John looked up the hill for a good five minutes. He knew what to say, and he knew what that information symbolized, but he didn't want to be the one to say it.

Turning around, he looked at Wilhem, who resignedly said, "We have to go around it!"

John nodded.

Jane dropping her full weight onto the sand, she said exasperatedly, "This can't be. I don't want to go back to that jungle!"

John looked at him, and taking his gaze to the jungle, he

understood Jane's fear. Everything that had happened when they entered the jungle was terrible. Going back in symbolized going through all that once more.

Not knowing that, he took a deep breath and looked at the ocean and said, "We could try swimming around!"

It was not a brilliant idea, but he would do anything not to enter the island again. Everyone looked at him in disbelief.

"We won't be able to swim around! There is only one way!" Haley said with fear in her eyes.

Wilhem took a deep breath as he placed his hand on the girl's shoulder when Jane, who wouldn't stop crying, stood up.

"Hate this damn island!" Jane said in between sobs.

Haley looked at her, and with some irritation in her mouth, she said, "Well, that's obvious! We all hate this place!"

Jane watched as Haley's tone of voice sounded reproachful, and walking a bit, she asked mockingly, "I cannot complain?"

Haley stared at her face when she said, "You can do whatever you want, Jane!"

And when she said that, she began to walk towards the island. As she advanced, Jane felt her irritation increase, and walking behind her, she said, "Yes, you can do whatever you want... I bet that's what your daddy says all the time!"

Haley looked at her reproachfully, and turning to face her, she said, "What does that have to do with our current situation?"

Jane took a deep breath when a roar was heard on the beach. Everyone jumped and, without narrowing the discussion, decided to advance through the forest. The sun was already in the sky, but the dense jungle created enormous shadows that did not allow the young people to see the path they were following correctly. They were all advancing trying to reach a point, when suddenly a sound paralyzed them.

John looked in all directions and slowly approached a tree, he asked cautiously, "Maybe it was an animal?"

But Jane, looking at him, fearfully said, "Have you seen an animal since we got here?"

John shook his head as he tried to think positive.

"They ate them all... we better keep walking. I want to get to the ship as soon as possible!" Jane suggested, her expression terrified.

Everyone nodded when right in the middle of the group, one of the creatures fell. His sharp teeth seemed to smile, and his long limbs fell parallel to his body. He had moved with such speed that none of the group realized he was in front of them until he fell right next to them.

Fear paralyzed them all, and Haley, trying to walk slowly to get away, looked at Wilhem. Both shared a look as they slowly walked away. John imitated his movement and marked his steps. He walked slowly to reach the flat side of the jungle and begin the escape.

All terrified felt their heart-pounding when Jane looked at the creature back and did not move the slightest muscle.

The girl was completely paralyzed, and despite the signs that her friends made, she simply looked directly at the back of the creature without being able to move.

Her breathing increased constantly, and her eyes were tearing without her being able to blink. The creature looked in the direction of nowhere while Jane felt like her heart was about to leave her chest.

At that moment, two hands took her, one covered her mouth, and the other pulled her tightly. As she turned her head, she looked at Haley, who had come back for her, calmly both began to move away, trying to make as little noise as possible when little by little, they advanced.

The creature did not seem to notice her movement, and for some reason, it did not move from the place where they were when he stretched out his arm to take Jane's bag without moving his body. The young woman let out a scream that was drowned out by the force of Haley's hand over her mouth.

She was breathing with such force that it seemed she was going to explode when Haley very carefully made her take her bag out and leave it in the hand of the creature, who still did not move.

They both took a couple more steps forward, and when they were on firmer ground, the creature turned its face and roared with full force.

Before that roar, the whole group began to run at full speed.

“Run! Run! Run!”

John screamed at the top of his lungs as he led the way through the jungle. It was difficult to advance, but he was trying his best to avoid obstacles and lead the way when he crossed a bush and fell face-first into a stream when in a jump.

Getting up with difficulty, he saw how his friends arrived and took a deep breath.

“Everyone is ok?” John asked worriedly.

Everyone nodded except Jane, who was looking at them in daze. Suddenly, she lost her balance and fell into the stream completely unconscious.

***

CHAPTER 14

The march through the forest was heavy. All the soldiers maintained a steady pace that Max had a hard time following. He was not particularly out of shape, but following the soldiers down the shaky path with the pressure of being attacked at any time was hard enough for him.

In his mind, the idea of lingering was terrifying. Even in flat daylight, that would be a disaster, he knew how difficult the situation was, and the idea of being alone in the middle of the forest with those creatures hanging around raised the thorn of his spine.

His arm began to feel tense and numb again. When he had left the forest and was with his friends on the beach, the influence of the island on his arm had ceased, but as they got closer and closer to the island bridge, everything got complicated more and more.

Suddenly Ashfaq raised his fist, stopping all his soldiers on the spot, Max who was in the center of the platoon, saw how all the soldiers raised their weapons ready to fight, everyone's gaze was intimidating, but despite their training and their clear The propensity to defend oneself The fear in the eyes of all those people was quite palpable.

Max was looking in all directions, and a powerful roar was heard quite far from his direction. The creatures seemed to be in the back, and the cry was nothing more than a warning that they would begin to chase their prey. Max felt terror creep up his spine.

“Sergeant! How are you on explosives?” Ashfap asked with a grin

The man opened his backpack and, shaking his head, said, “I only have one load, sir!”

Ashfaq took a deep breath. He was feeling resigned. “Put them in the deepest part of our trail, and don't clean the tracks! That load will at least make them move slower!”

The man obeyed and took the remaining carcasses from his backpack, and he prepared to perform the trap. Everyone watched in all directions while the man diligently worked.

Max looked at him with some admiration when he felt a hand on his shoulder that said, “Soon, we will have to talk about your role in this community! If you are not useful, I have no intention of taking you with me!”

Max felt Ashfaq's words fall on his body, it was a truth that he had to face but his mind hardly strayed from the numbness of his arm. When the man finished planting the trap, all the soldiers moved again. Max had appreciated the rest but returning to action showed him how sore his legs were and how terrible this situation could be.

As he advanced slowly, he felt the heat in his arm

increase, it was a subtle pain but capable of distracting him, and by squeezing his hand, he felt the heat increase rapidly. The soldiers did not stop, and no one seemed to be completely clear what they should do when suddenly the heat in his arm turned over and began to burn him deeply, but in the distance, a huge explosion sounded.

All the soldiers raised their weapons and pointed to the rear, the explosion was clearly the trap that the soldier had planted, and now they were attentive to their pursuers. At that moment, Max was looking at his hand. The pain was rapidly diminishing again.

Ashfaq looked towards the rising smoke screen, and smiling, he said, "Good job, Sergeant!"

The sergeant nodded, seriously.

Then Ashfaq noticed that Max was acting weird, Max was staring at his hands for who knows who long now.

"What's wrong, kid?" Ashfaq could not help but ask.

Max looked at him and said anxiously, "I think I can feel the creatures…"

He spoke without thinking, it was a sudden discovery, and that puzzled him. In the position he was in, that was an invaluable skill, and Ashfaq knew it perfectly.

Ashfaq looked at Max carefully. He came closer, before he asked, "What do you mean, you can feel them?"

But at that moment, Max felt how his mind was distracted, the heat in his arm began to rise with great force, and his pain became quite noticeable, the boy instinctively looked in one direction.

Ashfaq followed his gaze. “Soldiers to the right prepare for contact!”

All the soldiers raised their weapons, and at that moment, a wounded creature emerged from the dense jungle. All the soldiers fired in unison, causing his shots to open the creature's chest, it screamed and roared without stopping his advance, but the soldiers' shots made it slow down.

While the rain of shots fell on his chest, the creature watched Max, who, as he fell to the ground dead, felt how the constant heat of his arm diminished. He was right. The heat warned him of the vicinity of the creatures, which was an extremely useful skill.

But at that moment, he could only cover his ears because of the thunderous sound of weapons. He was not used to hearing them roar and seeing the creature's flesh jump in all directions as its body shattered under the constant nibbling of firearms. It made his stomach turn.

Two soldiers were there erred and began to shoot straight at the monster's skull unceremoniously, pieces of its skull and brains flying everywhere sticking to the pants of the soldiers who, with frantic smiles, did not stop enjoying while they finished with the creature.

Max could barely hold his urge to vomit when seeing Ashfaq. He watched him smile. Max could not understand what attracted them to that enormous amount of violence. Clearly, the creature was dead when the shots stopped. Little more than a mass of blood and brains were left. Everyone enjoyed and congratulated themselves on that terrible reality.

Max looked at them, and in his mind, it was difficult to see who the monsters were or if any of them in that place were human. Ashfaq looked at him, and taking his shirt made him stand up. The boy could barely bear the smell of gunpowder and visors, and the vision was even gloomier.

When Ashfaq looked at him, Max tried to keep his composure, but a firm, hard hit to the stomach made everything in him come to his mouth. As he tried to breathe, he could feel like he was vomiting forcefully, and his hands fell on the wet floor when he saw the contents of his intestines.

He tried to get up when a kick made him fall sideways near where the remains of the creature were. Max dragged himself with force to walk away when he looks at the officer at hand crouching in front of him.

"What's up, kid?! This is disgusting to you?" Ashfaq asked unhappily.

Max felt his eyes fill with tears. He was terrified.

"I thought you wanted a treasure! That you wanted to be an explorer!" Ashfaq continued to rebuke.

His eyes penetrated his gaze. Max did not want to see him, he just wanted to sit for a second and feel the enormous amount of sensations that overwhelmed him, but that was not possible.

The man in front of him did not have the slightest trace of

compassion. At that moment, a roar in the distance made him shudder if they weren't the target only another group on the island could be.

Ashfaq crouched in front of him looked in the direction that the distant roar was felt. Getting up, he took the radio before saying looking directly at Max.

“It's time to get the tough little boy! Or that could be you!” When he said that, he started to walk and said, “We don't have all day! Ladies, move!”

Before moving forward, he looked at Max and said, “Every time you feel one of those bastards coming, tell me! Otherwise, I'll kill you! It seems we found your use!”

Max felt suffocated as the military began to walk. The image of the shattered creature turned his stomach. This situation was too much for him, but the only way to keep going was to make sure his friends were safe.

He could not afford to break in that situation, with no room to doubt standing up he said, “I will not die in this place!”

And walking, he followed the ball. At the front, Ashfaq kept the boy under surveillance when turning up the radio, he said, “Klivert, do you hear me? Over!”

After a few seconds, the radio answered, “Here, Klivert, over!”

Ashfaq let out a smile. For a minute, he had been worried that that strange roar was the end of his partner, but calmly he said, “Do you have any information!?”

The radio took a second to ring, and with a small noise of interference, Ashfaq heard the voice of his man.

"That boy is fuller of shit than the latrines of the camp over!"

Ashfaq looked at Max, who was walking at a calm pace when he said, “Then the little rat lied!”

"That's right, Commander!" Klivert said on the radio, "His friends didn't let him! He left them on his trail. His friends are just as immersed in this shit as we are. I'll follow the trail and secure them along with an alternate exit route over! "

Ashfaq did not like to be lied to, and he was a spiteful man upon hearing that he said, “It's okay! Continue with the order! And when you find them, kill one ... that will teach that brat not to lie to me!”

The radio gave the affirmative and then fell silent. Ashfaq looked at Max as he approached and said, “Brat, are you sure your friends left the island?”

Max jumped and looked that man in the eye, he said, “Yes! It is most likely!”

Ashfaq held his gaze for a second, and then nodding, he said, “Everything is fine! Everybody move!”

The road was still long, and Max had not felt the proximity of the creatures again. The expedition had reached a river where everyone took some water just for one of them to say, “Brat! How did you know the monster was near?”

Max looked at him, and it seemed that his question was

genuine, and he was drinking water from the river and feeling a deep hunger, he said carefully, "I felt it..."

The guy nodded as he ate his portion. He was a clearly young blond man. He seemed confused about the whole situation, but still, his gaze did not show anger.

Instead, he seemed to have great curiosity when he said, "When I saw them! I thought they were like zombies, you know? They bite you, and you transform! But nah, it's not like that."

Max looked at him confused.

The guy continued, "Zombies are slow and dumb! These bastards are so fast!"

"I've never seen a Zombie in the Jungle movie," Another one of the soldiers sitting next to the boy said, "Have you seen any?"

Max shook his head slowly. The calm with which the soldiers remained impressed him, the guy next to him looked at him for a long time and smiled and said, "If not for you! Many would have died!" Saying that he took a protein bar and gave it to the boy.

Max took it somewhat confused and, looking at him, said, "My stomach is upset..."

The soldier smiled and looked at the man in front of him who, from a bag, took out a small white vial and said, "Drink this boy."

Max took a sip of the medicine, and the bitter taste of it

seemed to calm his nausea instantly. Feeling the well-being of he took a strong drink, and the relief intensified.

Looking at the bottle distractedly, the man said with a smile, “Military medicine, son.”

Everyone seemed to be comfortable with the boy, and Max looked at them with confusion and heard one more said, “If the boy senses them approaching, we can defend ourselves! Then we defend the boy!”

Max nodded slowly. Unsure what to feel about the current situation.

“What is this? A social gathering? Let's move, ladies!” Ashfaq said in anger.

They all nodded and got up. The man who had given him the protein bar offered him a hand and helped him up.

Once on his feet, he said, “Keep me safe, and I keep you safe!”

And taking his rifle, he blinked his eye, the others patted Max's back, and everyone began to walk calmly, his new ability could give him certain advantages, and it was clear that everyone saw it. Perhaps Max was not as helpless as he thought he was.

***

CHAPTER 15

John and Wilhem carried Jane after she lost consciousness. Staying in that place was not an option. Neither knew what was happening with the girl, but they assumed that it was an excess of fear that led her to fall unconscious while carrying her. They were trying to flee from the roaring creature, but at that moment, a loud explosion sounded far in the distance.

"Did you hear that?" Haley asked in fear.

John watched as the cloud of black smoke grew above the trees and understood instantly that it was Ashfaq's group.

"We must go! Fast!" John said trying to decide if it would be but to fall into the hands of the soldiers or the creatures in either case would they survive. "Let's continue down the path!"

Wilhem and John were putting all their strength into carrying an unconscious Sam when Haley, looking in all directions, somehow began to survey the terrain. She walked confidently.

She looked at her friends and said, "Follow me! In this direction!"

Without raising an interfering voice, John decided to follow her. A few meters from the stream, they both arrived again at the village where everything had begun. Wilhem and John put Jane carefully on the floor as they looked around her. Both smiled, looking at each other and raising his hand for the other to bump it just to see how Jane regained consciousness.

“Are you okay?” Wilhem asked with unmasked worry.

The girl opened her eyes and looked around her. She immediately recognized the village, and a relieved smile appeared on her face as tears fell from her face.

Haley was looking in all directions for the way to get to the boat, and when she found it, she shed a tear as she said, “Boys, I found the way!”

But before they could respond, two strong arms grabbed her, and closing her mouth, they drew her towards the large body of a man. At first, she thought it was a creature.

Closing her eyes tightly, she waited for imminent death, but realizing that this was not the situation, she opened her eyes to see who was holding her. Against all odds, she observed Ory.

She was shaking herself free from her grasp when she asked, “What's wrong?”

But the man only raised his hands, pointing to one place.

Haley turned her head, John and Wilhem who also did the same to see where the man was pointing at.

Sam slowly stood up, and just above him, a blackish-skinned, muddy man-shaped creature landed.

He thought about turning, but a hand bigger than that of an average man took his neck from the back and, preventing his movement, stopped him in place.

Sam tried to squirm or move, but the force of the creature lifted him off the ground so that his feet did not touch the surface of the earth, he was gasping for air, and Wilhem near him trying to retaliate but saw no progress, John making a hasty decision, took Wilhem by the hand and held him.

He pulled towards where Haley was. Wilhem tried to resist only to see how Sam raised his hand begging for help, but the help would not come. The cannibal's arm pierced his abdomen with such force that part of his blood fell on Wilhem's body.

Sam began to ooze blood while his body writhed in pain and as if his speech was restored, a scream of anguish sounded throughout the jungle. The cannibal opened his jaw to all that it gave and biting the guy's neck tore a huge piece of his flesh, thereby taking the life out of the young man in the same way.

Wilhem, disgusted by the image, continued to feel the pull of John, who was leading him in the direction of Haley and the boatman who had already started the flight. As they ran, they could hear the cannibal's feast as he ate the remains of his friend, who no longer had any hope.

The race did not last long when they reached the beach

where the boat was anchored. Ory continued dragging Haley while John and Wilhem tried to assimilate what happened while they saw the boatman.

"We have to help Sam! He may be alive!" The young woman said frantically.

But the guy was not paying any attention to her request. John saw how he dragged her without delicacy, and moving forward, he broke the hold he had on Haley and, seeing him said, "You have to help us rescue Sam!"

"Don't be a stupid kid!" The boatman replied, "Are you blind? H already died! And if we don't leave, now we will die too!"

John wanted to argue, but a voice that didn't belong to either of them sounded from the side.

"No one is going anywhere in this place!"

Ory, behind his pants, pulled out a revolver and pointed dircctly at the man who appeared.

Klivert was pointing his rifle back at him when he said,"Put that down old man! I don't want you to get hurt!"

Ory, with a penetrating look, said, "I'm like a fucking surgeon with this thing! If you don't want to get into trouble, you better go with your squad!"

Klivert moved a little further, and pointed at the girl, and then asked expressionlessly, "What if I shoot her?"

Haley saw the barrel of the gun in her direction, and her hand raised terrified as Ory raised his.

“No! It's okay! Don't hurt the lady!”

Haley saw him surprised. She did not know why that man suddenly decided to give up, but it was clear that his interest in her was high. Ory saw the confusion on the young woman's face and said, "I'm a sorry lady! Your father is my boss! He asked me to protect you! "

She was going to ask a question, but before that happened, Klivert, moving forward, said, “What a bad job you did, old man!”

And with those words, he fired two shots straight to Ory's head. The man fell dead to the ground instantly, and his revolver fell to the sand.

At that moment, Klivert pointed to everyone else and calmly said, “Get on the boat! Nobody leaves! We will all wait together in that place!”

The youngsters slowly obeyed when Klivert took the radio to warn his partner that he already had the boys.

On the other side of the island, several confrontations had already happened. Still, Max's ability to know when the creatures were approaching was extraordinary, he kept the soldiers on guard, and they could fight with the creatures.

In a matter of hours, they had reached the camp once there. Ashfaq looked at all his supplies and, looking at his men, said, “Boys! Time to arm yourself! We will catch these creatures!”

Max noticed that Ashfaq had no intention of leaving the island or simply killing the monsters. He just wanted to catch them, which made him angry.

He knew that he needed to find a better way to act when at that moment, a vision triggered.

Max was again in a dark space.

The mountain loomed in front of him. It was as if he knew the whole island perfectly when the ancient king appeared and said, *"It's time! The ritual of capturing the creatures will be launched! You just have to get to the south side of the mountain, at the entrance of the sun! There is the ritual that I set up. It gets there, and as my chosen one spills blood in the bowl as a sacrifice and the creatures will be caught forever!"*

Max woke up from his trance. He then realized that in front of him was Ashfaq.

Ashfaq looked at him with interest. He approached him and asked, "You had a vision, didn't you?" Saying that with a smile, he asked, "What did you see?"

Max thought of lying, but the heat of his arm intensified, he thought of telling the soldiers. Still, he saw it as an opportunity and kept his silence.

***

CHAPTER 16

Max looked Ashfaq directly in the eyes, and he was about to lie to maintain his status when the heat of his arm rose uncontrollably. He knew instantly that the attack was imminent, and his instinct told him that they would come from everywhere.

The Ashfaq soldiers watched their interaction without imagining for a second the imminent attack that was coming upon them.

Max kept his gaze steady on the commander's eyes when he asked, “What's wrong, kid? Tell me, what did you see?”

The pain in his arm was very severe. The heat almost spread all over his face. When looking right over Ashfaq's shoulder, he saw how one of the creatures came out of the jungle tearing off the head of one of the soldiers.

Ashfaq heard the shots and saw as the creatures began to emerge from all directions. That was all it took for him to realize that Max had deliberately let them get to them.

Turning his gaze, he looked for Max with his eyes which started to run towards the jungle. Ashfaq chased him, catching up with him in a matter of seconds when kicking him. He threw him to the ground while he took his pistol and pointed at the boy's face.

Max's eyes widened when one of the creatures ran in his direction. The commander raised the pistol, and Max took advantage of that distraction to resume his flight. He got up as best he could from the muddy ground and began to run in the direction of the jungle, the shots and the roars were everywhere without stopping. The new weapons made an appearance, raising explosions in all directions.

Ashfaq, who had endured the attack of one of the creatures, took the grenade launcher. He was not willing to allow Max to escape, and pointing in his direction, he prepared to shoot. Still, before he could do it, his soldiers shot, and the explosion made him move his sight just before pulling the trigger.

The grenade landing on Max's side not close enough to hurt him, but the shock wave from the explosion lifted him off the ground, causing him to fall into the thick jungle in pain. His mind spun as he felt the muddy ground on his face. He tried to get up but was finding it difficult to breathe from the impact when he felt a roaring pass near him.

Getting up as best he could, he observed how the severed limbs of one of the soldiers fell in front of him when a creature saw him. Max knew immediately that that creature had placed him as a target, and running at full speed, he entered the jungle.

Fear had given him a vigor that he did not know. He ran

through the jungle, trying to escape from his pursuer at full speed. He ran without stopping while overcoming obstacles and trying to avoid all difficulties.

But not far from him, he could hear the advance of the creature trying to give him a hunt. As he ran, he took the courage to look at his back and saw how the obstacles that he was clearing the creature ignored with his incredible strength, chasing the young man at all speed.

Max did not want to be caught and increased his speed as the creature approached to give it a final blow. He evaded by ducking just in time to then try to jump a branch and fall short. His feet collided with one of those branches, and falling face down, he rolled down the hill until he fell into a deep river. The creature chased him, but the river was very deep, and when he did not feel his feet under it, the creature lost control of its movements.

Max was never too athletic, but he could swim as well as anyone, and moving away from that beast until he reached the other shore, he watched as the creature came out of the water to mount on the other shore. When it saw him, it let out a scream full of anger and ran around the edge. Max knew that now the hunt for him was personal.

Without staying to contemplate it, he began to run at full speed, trying to escape from the creature. The distance he had gained was enough for him to maintain a steady pace, and from his vision, he had a total understanding of the island. Reaching the king's village was no problem as he was not following the path until he reached the ship. For a minute, he saw it and couldn't believe his luck. If his friends were with him, without a doubt, he would be able to escape at once from that place.

He advanced quickly to get to the ship when he saw the corpse of Ori on the ground next to a revolver. When he saw it, he knew that something was not right. He bent down and took the revolver just before walking down the destroyed dock until he reached the boat. Once on it, he looked on the deck and saw his friends sitting on the ground tight up.

Everyone saw him and his eyes lit up. He was confused when he was going to speak when he heard a voice from above the booth.

“You are the brat who was with Ashfaq! You're going to explain to me right now why the hell they won’t answer the radio!”

Max looked directly at the face of Klivert, who was pointing his rifle at him. Max had thought it very strange that he had not been on the expedition, but it was too late to get used to that idea, looking at his enemy, he said, “We were attacked by a lot of creatures! I don’t know why they don't answer. I could hardly escape!”

When he said that, he felt a little heat on his arm and knew that the creature was approaching. Calmly but feigning urgency, he said, “One of the soldiers escaped with me, but he's wounded, he's close, I couldn't save him!”

Max could see the clear concern on Klivert's face, who went down while pointing at him and then asked, “Where?!”

“In the village! I really couldn't bring it!” He said as he turned and pointed to the village.

As he said that, the heat in his arm increased more and more. Klivert advanced and, looking at him, before asking mockingly, “Do you think you can fool me, child?”

Max opened his eyes in surprise when Klivert hit his stomach hard. Max fell to the ground completely in pain, writhing, trying to find air to breathe.

When he looked at Klivert said, “I'm not lying to you!”

The soldier raised the rifle and pointed it and said, “Shut your mouth, you damn brad!”

But at that moment in the jungle, the creature that was hunting Max appeared. When Klivert saw it, he felt fear rise up his back and, taking his rifle, began to shoot desperately in his direction.

The shots couldn't stop the creature, which leaped up and grabbed onto the edge of the ship.

“They can't swim!” Max yelled from the floor.

Klivert heard that, and with full force, he threw himself on the creature and, placing the barrel of his rifle in his face, shot several times. The force of the shots made the creature fall into the water Klivert looked at him, twisting on the water, and Max pulled the hammer of the revolver behind him. Klivert heard how a gun was triggered, but before he could react, the shot shattered his head, and it fell into the water.

Max ran to his friends and released the hug. Everyone has

reunited again. Wilhem hugged him while Haley cried, and John stood up. Max looked with his eyes and did not find Sam.

"Where is Sam?!" He questioned in panic.

But no one could answer. Max shook his head and, looking at Haley, said, "Ory, he's dead! I saw his corpse outside on the beach!" As he said that, he looked at John and said, "We must get off this damn island at once!"

John nodded, but the creature's arm pierced his friend's chest from the ship's rail. Max and the rest of his friends watched him stunned as the monster standing on the edge lifted John up into the air as his blood rushed out of the hollow in his chest.

At that moment and without stopping, the creature embedded the other arm, crossing the boy with both hands and separating him into two parts, causing his torso to become a piece and his legs to fall into the boat with the guts dripping.

The creature bit into one of John's body fragments as the boy's head fell overboard. With his gaze full of anger and his teeth reddened from the bite of his friend's bleeding body, the creature roared with total power, ready to end the lives of everyone else when a bullet hit him. Fragment seconds later, his body exploded in several pieces.

Max's eyes widened when he saw that spectacle when three men with emaciated faces and robes full of blood climbed into the boat.

One of them was a damaged Ashfaq who, looking at Max,

said, “Damn child! Did you think you could get rid of me?”

And with those words, he raised the gun to point Max straight at his face. Max's arms were sore, and looking at his pursuer, he could only raise his hands and knew his escape from the island would not be so immediate.

***

CHAPTER 17

Ashfaq pointed directly at Max's face as he advanced.

Max in a quick movement, handed the revolver to one of his friends without Ashfaq noticing.

"I know you're upset—"

But before Max could say more, Ashfaq hit his face so hard that he fell to the ground abruptly. Max felt his head vibrate.

As he tried to get up, he felt another kick hit his ribs, his oxygen leaving his lungs as he crawled hard to stop and get air. He tried to look at one of his friends, but another kick sent him rolling across the deck.

The military man was angry and, looking at the boy, laughed as he said, "All my soldiers are dead because of you!"

When he said that, he gave him another kick that made him release the oxygen even more. From above, I saw him squirming, and at that moment, he said, "You are going to die, in this place!"

Wilhem thought about taking out the revolver and starting to shoot, maybe they would have a chance, but they would surely die instantly. The two soldiers who were with Ashfaq pointed at them with determination.

When Ashfaq hit him hard once more, Max raised his hand, pointing directly towards the mountain. Ashfaq looked at the gesture, and a hint of curiosity rose through his body. He looked at the mountain and then looked at the sore child, he said, “What do you have to tell me?! You are a disgusting brat!”

Max took a few seconds to catch his breath. When looking at Ashfaq, he looked straight at the mountain and said, “The vision I had... it showed me a ritual of how to control beasts!”

Max found himself lying with ease, and as he looked into the military's eyes, he knew right away that his intrigue had intensified.

Looking at his men, they were terrified when he said, “That would be the chance that we could move on!”

The two soldiers did not look too comfortable with the idea but opposing Ashfaq did not seem the most brilliant action. Both soldiers nodded when looking at Max.

“You will guide there, kid!” Ashfaq said.

Max gritted his teeth. With great difficulty he managed to stand up. “You have to promise nothing will happen to my friends!”

Ashfaq stared at him and, nodding, said, “Okay!” Then looking directly at Wilhem and Haley, he continued with a weird smile, “I agree with you. But, by the way, Boy or girl!?”

Max, confused. He looked at him, completely unable to understand what he meant.

“Boys or girls!” Ashfaq repeated. But before Max would even speak, the man added, “Well, it doesn't really matter.”

Just as he said that, Ashfaq raised his pistol and shot Wilhem in the stomach.

Max screamed, and immediately crawled towards his friend. Wilhem was bleeding from his mouth, and in his last breaths, he looked at Haley with a smile.

Haley cried hard and Wilhem between tears he touched her face with his bloody hand.

Max couldn't believe what had happened. He furiously said, “What the fuck?! Why did you do that?!”

But Ashfaq, hitting him very hard in the face, said, “It's not fair that your men survive and mine doesn't!”

When he said that, he raised the gun to point it at Haley, who was also terrified. Ashfaq looked at Max with a mad grin, “You still have a friend here! If you want to save her, do what I told you!”

Max nodded forcefully. He stepped in front of Haley trying to protect her.

Ashfaq looked at him with a smile and, seeing one of his men, said, “You will stay in this boat! You'll keep it ready to go when we get back! Taking care of the girl, if she does something dumb, kill her!”

The man looked at the girl and, nodding, released a nasty smile. Max looked at Haley. Her gaze was completely terrified while she was still holding the dying Wilhem. His blood kept coming out, and with firm eyes on Max, the boy nodded.

Max angrily began to walk while the commander and his only remaining soldier followed him with pistol force. They ran at full speed towards the south side of the island where the vision had taught Max how to seal the creatures. He had to find a way to get rid of Ashfaq and go back to rescue Haley, but that would be really difficult.

While he was climbing the mountain, several creatures attacked them. Still, with Max's ability, they were able to repel them as they advanced at full speed. In less than an hour, they managed to reach the southern entrance of the mountain. We're walking at full speed, they began to climb.

“Damn!” Ashfaq cursed, going up the path that clearly appeared, “So on the side where he was looking! The damn monsters were there. I should have always looked around here!”

Max climbed with them very closely. The closer he got, the more his arm ached instinctively. He knew he was close and could feel the creatures moving around the island. The presence of the dead king was even stronger in that place, and he could almost hear his voice.

As they advanced, he saw a huge cave, he knew perfectly well that it was the right place, and when he saw it, he said, “He's in that place, but I must go in alone!”

Ashfaq looked at him and forcefully kicked his stomach again, Max fell to the ground without being able to breathe.

When he saw it, the commander said, "You're an asshole if you think I'll fall for that!"

He then lifted the boy by the shoulder and, looking at his subordinate, said, "You will stay protecting this entrance if something happens and I don't go out! Kill this damn kid! And he kills her friend only after raping her ten times, is that clear!"

The soldier nodded, and Max wasn't sure, but he thought he saw a strange pleasure on his face. At that moment, he and Ashfaq entered the cave.

Wilhem was still dying in Haley's arms on the ship, who, seeing him, said, "I'm very sorry about this!"

As she said that, her tears fell on her friend when she hugged him from her raised her head, and asked, "Do you want water?"

Wilhem nodded, and she looked at the soldier, said, "Can I give him water?"

The soldier, with a half-smile, nodded when the young woman got up and walked to the cabin to get the water. He took her by her hair and threw her to the ground with force.

He looked at her, and smiling, he asked full of sarcasm, "Why wastewater on a dead man?"

She cried when she saw him try to stand up and pointed his gun at the girl.

“I've been on this damn island for a long time...” As he said that, he was running his lips over his mouth, and looking at Haley with heated desire.

“And you'll be here a lot more damn pig!” Haley yelled.

The man widened his eyes in surprise when a shot sounded behind him, and his back was where the shot hit. He turned around to watch Wilhem using his last moments to shoot him.

The shot staggered the soldier, letting go of his rifle only for him to pull out his handgun from his holster and fire three more times at the young man's body. When he did, this Haley got up with speed and, using Wilhem's razor, stabbed the soldier in the back.

The man dropped the gun, but he was a very big and strong man, and turning with force, he hit Haley with his elbow making her fall to the ground. He tried to remove the knife, but he took his own knife and looked at the young woman he said when he did not reach it, “I'm going to cut you up, you damn brat!”

“I don't think you can make it, fucker!” Haley had crawled over to his rifle.

And taking his rifle, she raised the barrel straight to the man's chest and, pulling the trigger, let out a blast that destroyed the soldier's torso making him fall overboard. When the man fell dead, she ran to Wilhem, but her friend had already passed away. Unable to avoid it, the girl burst into tears.

Ashfaq and Max entered the cave together. They both

walked, seeing the drawings and the strange ornate vessels. Max looked in all directions and, for some reason, knew everything that had to happen in that place and what was happening at that moment.

He went to the altar where the ritual had to take place and said, “I must put my blood in that bowl, then you will! Then the control will be yours!”

Max looked at Ashfaq and the military man taking the knife said, “Take it! If you try something phony, I'll blow your head off!”

Max nodded, and taking the knife, he stood in front of the altar, and his arm began to burn uncontrollably. Cutting his hand, he threw a little blood on the bowl and heard the words in his mind.

An unknown language that, for some reason, he could speak perfectly.

“Ajacmirasagario!”

A small tremor opened a room next to him, and all the treasures of the island appeared in that place. Max looked at the treasure and the reason why his friends were dead, and he cried.

Ashfaq looked at it and walked to admire it. Seeing the distraction, Max took the knife in his hand, and with force, he embedded it in the soldier's back. He let out a yell only to turn hard and kick the boy in the abdomen that knocked him down.

Taking the rifle, he aimed at the boy, and annoyed he said,

“This time, I'll kill you!”

But while he said that, two huge arms crossed his chest, the rifle fell to the ground while Ashfaq looked at Max. He could not believe what he saw. A huge number of creatures praised the soldier with force and destroyed his body while they fed on him, biting his back.

Max approached with an impulse of courage. He took the rifle from the ground and, approaching Ashfaq's body, haloed one of the grenade rings, activating it as he said.

“Fuck you bastard! This is for Wilhem!” and with those words, he fled while Ashfaq's body exploded into pieces.

Running at full speed, the soldier at the entrance was about to see what happened when a hail of shots from inside the door knocked him down. The man was bleeding on the ground when he watched as Max shot out of the cave.

Behind him, various creatures began to chase him, the roars on the island became more and more present, activating the retention spell made all the creatures in that place perceive that it was the beginning of the end. Max running at full speed, the creatures tried to cut off his path to eliminate him.

They were all very strong, but their speed and reaction were considerably stopped due to the spell. With speed, Max ran at all he gave when the creatures began to appear from his sides. He could not follow his path back to the ship, and taking an alternative escape, he reached a path that overlooked a cliff.

He began to run while one of the creatures struck him on the back and opened a wound, stopping he ran leaning on the ground leaving blood marks from the wound on his hand that did not stop bleeding, the edge of the cliff was close when one of the female creatures managed to catch him and bite his shoulder. At the same time, he jumped without stopping into the ocean.

The fall was immediate, but when he fell into the water, the creature released him, he swam as he could and looking weak he could not imagine how he will survive when a rope came to him, taking it he looked up and saw how Haley was pulling him, Max did everything he could to get on the boat.

She was pulling with all her might on Max's aching body until they both fell into the boat. Once inside, a light rose in the sky, and the creatures on the island that were still roaring began to retreat. Max sitting down was breathing with difficulty when Haley hugged him crying.

All his friends were dead, only they had survived.

"They are all dead, Max!"

"Not all!" Max said, shedding a few tears. "You and I are not. Thanks to them, we are saved!"

Both of them stayed in that place for a second while the ship floated in the water. Still, a creature clung to one side of its hull, one of those monsters of the island in the form of a woman that seemed to be about to give birth.

The nightmare was far from over. Instead, it would grow even bigger.

www.ingramcontent.com/pod-product-compliance
Lightning Source LLC
LaVergne TN
LVHW041109150826
845673LV00007B/1984

* 9 7 9 8 4 8 1 0 9 6 1 4 8 *